The Least of It

Peter Nash

Fomite
Burlington, VT

ISBN-13: 978-1-953236-08-1
Library of Congress Control Number: 2021941474
Fomite
58 Peru Street
Burlington, VT 05401
www.fomitepress.com
10/26/2021

For Annie, Ezra, and Isaiah

For JPW

What happened is the least of it.

~Javier Marías

I MET MY FRIEND ARSÈNE, the psychiatrist, in front of
Casa Luis Barragán in the old Tacubaya neighborhood
of Mexico City at precisely 10 a.m. on the morning
of June 3rd. It was warm, a Tuesday. We'd planned to
get there early, so as to have a little time to talk before
devoting our attention to our guide, a young man, a
student and poet named Alberto Juárez with whom
I'd spoken on the telephone the day before. There on
Calle Generalissimo Francisco Ramírez, a quiet dead-
end street in Colonia Daniel Garza, I found my friend
reading a slender red volume in Spanish about another
architect and engineer, the exiled Spaniard, Félix
Candela Outeriño, best known for his development of
thin shells of reinforced concrete called cascarones. It
was about cascarones, and about the architectural use
of reinforced concrete in general, that we found ourselves talking at once, without preamble that morning,
indeed with scarcely a word of greeting, though I'd had

every intention of asking him about his recently married daughter, Élise, of whom I am fond, and about the book he was writing, a pet project on the madness of Charlotte of Belgium, or Carlota, the wife of the hapless Mexican emperor, Maximilian I. He was full of ideas, my friend, in fact so excited about the book on Candela he was reading, and about the many things he wished to tell me since the last time we met, that I little suspected that three days later he would hang himself with an electrical cord in his apartment here in Condesa.

He'd been visiting Mexico City for more than twenty years, first for a week, to stay with a cousin, a painter in Del Valle, then for a month, a summer, then for a period of nearly three years, following his divorce from my childhood friend, Simin, for me a gaping, vacant spell in his life during which he'd worked as a psychiatric consultant at the Instituto Nacional de Psiquiatría Dr. Ramón de la Fuente Muñiz, while conducting his own lifelong research on major depressive disorder, specifically on brain metabolism and oxidative stress, neither of which he'd ever bothered to explain to me, preferring always, whenever we met, to speak of other, at most tangentially related things.

Not once had we communicated during that time, what must have been a dark and lonely period for him. I'd been so preoccupied with my work, and with my father's failing health, a degenerative nervous disease from which he'd suffered in silence for years, that I can't remember ever even having thought of Arsène, except perhaps vaguely, as in relation to someone or something else, a fact not unusual in our long and variable relationship. Since meeting as students in New York, when for a time we'd been inseparable, briefly sharing an apartment above a Turkish restaurant in Greenwich Village, we'd passed in and out of each other's lives with a fluid, nearly musical regularity, so that I'd had no idea he was even here in Mexico City, that Simin had left him, that he'd confronted her at last, he must have, she must have told him everything, simply going through the motions of my life each day as if nothing in our relationship had changed. How little I'd known! How smug my assumption that, while my own fortunes had shifted almost daily, his life (at least the life I'd always ascribed to him) had remained blissfully, reliably the same.

Yet such habits die hard, for despite all he'd been through (most of which I'd only surmised), he seemed very much the same that day, at Casa Barragán, emphatically so—the same bright eyes, the same wide grin, the same fast affection for me, which he expressed in a host of warm, unwitting ways: by cocking his head to the right, by biting his lip, by squeezing my arm as we walked. Still I couldn't help wondering what he knew, that is, *how much*, and studied him with a restless agitation. It was not like him to dissemble, to mask his thoughts and feelings: all the more reason to beware.

He was eager to tell me about a trip he'd just taken to see Candela's famous chapel, Capilla Lomas de Cuernavaca, on the wide flat plain outside the city there, a city he loved especially, and to which, years earlier, we'd traveled together to see the collection at the Brady Museum.

On this occasion, he'd felt the need to make the trip there alone, he told me frankly, if with no attempt to explain himself, taking me by the arm and guiding me to the end of the quiet dead-street, past an old woman selling tlacoyos, then up onto a narrow, graffiti-covered footbridge that crossed the busy Avenida Constituyentes, where briefly we stood speechless above the roaring traffic, above the interminable flood of trucks and cars and peseros, gazing out at the vast, hazy spectacle of the city, as though it were nothing but a dream, when with a chuckle, with a pat on my arm, he continued the story of his trip, speaking quickly, fervidly, of "object building", "force paths", and "free edges", and of the miraculous, if little-known development of ferroconcrete.

He was fascinated by Candela's use of the hyperbolic paraboloid in the design of his chapel, a subject upon which I asked him to elaborate, once we returned to the quiet, tree-lined street, where by then a half a dozen people had gathered before the museum entrance in the pale morning light, tourists all—a young Dutch couple, three architecture students from Taiwan, a bearded Swede in sandals, and an elderly man with a portable oxygen pack, a professor of English from Peru. It was the distinctive saddle shape of the building that had most intrigued my friend, he explained to me, as we strolled the other way down the lightly dappled street, a fascination that had inspired him to spend the better part of the day there on the empty grounds, patiently examining the strange, open-air structure from every vantage, every angle, ever more impressed, as the hours passed and the light around him changed, by the sheer audacity of its dimensions, its grace.

By coincidence he'd arrived here, in Mexico City, just days before I had, having been struck one morning, while working with a patient, by the need to get away. Excited by the thought of leaving New York, a city for which he'd lost his feeling, and by the advent of summer in Chapultepec Park, he'd rushed home, packed his things, then hurried to the airport, unlocking the door to his apartment here, some six hours later, where he'd poured himself a whiskey, then collapsed on the bed.

It was late the next morning, when he was looking for something to read with his coffee, that he'd chanced upon the slender red volume on Candela in a box of books that a friend had left for him. He'd been so taken with the architect, with his "umbrellas", with his fine, soaring "shells", that that very day he'd rushed off without eating to see for himself some of Candela's best-known works throughout the city: his rather disappointing Cosmic Rays Pavilion at the Universidad Nacional Autónoma de México; his covered market and Cavalier Industries Factory (formerly the High Life Textile Factory) in Coyoacán; his Iglesia de la Virgen de la Medalla Milagrosa in Narvarte; his metro station in Venustiano Carranza, with its folded hypar shells; and finally Los Manantiales, the popular restaurant he'd designed by the floating gardens of Xochimilco, known to locals as "La Flor".

He was happy to see me, pausing now and then to smile at me or to squeeze my arm, as if in apology for his ardor, his zeal, which often expressed itself in a storm, a blizzard of words.

He was dressed as usual that day in a rumpled green blazer, pale shirt, dark linen trousers, and a gray straw fedora, what in all might have seemed the trappings of a dandy, if I hadn't known better. For there was little of the fop about him; indeed, as ever, he seemed at odds with his clothes, fussing with his sleeves and tugging at his collar like a schoolboy at a wedding or wake.

He was perhaps a little paler than I remembered him, his hair thinner, his hands, his gestures, now fitful, now grave. A fine blue vein had surfaced near the edge of one eye. As we walked he held his hat in his hand, waving it about him as he spoke, so that the children on the next block stopped what they were doing to look at him.

He'd spent most of the night reading, he told me, reading and writing and making notes. As we strolled back and forth on the quiet, dead-end street, biding our time until our tour began, he told me about the recent revisions he'd made to the fourth and "finally critical" chapter of his book about the empress, changes inspired by his precipitate return to Mexico City, and by some letters he'd found included in an old German study of the Second French Intervention here, a book he'd discovered by chance the other day while browsing the dark, cluttered shelves of Librería

Regia, his favorite of the many old book shops on Calle Donceles.

The letters, four in all, comprised a brief, if revealing correspondence between a Doctor Jilek and an alienist in Vienna named Riedel. The first three, addressed by hand to Doctor Jilek at Miramare Castle, the Habsburg retreat near Trieste where the empress had been sequestered for her health, consisted largely of Riedel's analysis of her moods, which had grown erratic of late (he'd twice used the word beunruhigend), while the fourth, what at first had looked like a docket, a list, had been written by Carlota herself, in what had seemed a child's hand, a scrawling, nearly illegible missive in French (faithfully translated into German) in which, following a litany of complaints about the food, the servants, and the rain, she remarks upon her recent headaches and sleeplessness, and upon a terrible dream she'd had one night that her beloved Maximilian was dead.

Only when Arsène had talked himself out, his face flushed, the hair about his forehead damp with sweat, when at last we stood huddled with the others before the modest museum entrance, checking the time and shuffling our feet, only then did he tell me that his mother was dead. I'd met her once before, a brash, formidable woman, a scholar of modern Jewish history who'd died one night from an overdose of pills. There was no one else he could tell, he explained to me, as we crowded our way into the small, dark foyer of the museum, a remark I didn't understand, and to which I hadn't the time to reply, our guide commencing his tour of the house and studio at once with a brief biography of Barragán himself, citing his birth in Guadalajara in 1908, his training as a civil engineer and architect, and his travels, before the war, through Italy, Morocco, and Spain.

From there, from the foyer, we followed our guide up a short flight of steps into the startlingly pink central vestibule of the house, with its bright natural lighting and dark volcanic tiles, where (so we were told by our guide) the architect had liked to sit when he talked on the phone. Rather than mounting the central staircase at once, we made our way through what might have been the door to a bathroom or closet into the high-ceilinged living room, with its calm muted colors and wide glass view of the flowering overgrown garden he'd loved, then on through to his library-cum-study, with its books and sculptures and paintings, with its handsome L-shaped desk, where briefly we paused beneath the high reticulated window to marvel at his phonograph and records, and at his famous wooden staircase, suspended as if by magic against a bare white wall.

Yet what had impressed us most about the house (we'd agreed upon this at once) was his bedroom itself, the room in which he'd died, but a monk's cell, really, with its single bed, its reading chair, and its crucifix on the wall by his head. And we'd loved the brightly painted patio on the roof, with its hanging bougainvillea, its walls so high one could see nothing but sky.

IT WAS MY FRIEND'S IDEA, once the tour of the house was over, to walk to Chapultepec Park, a park which, in its spirit and beauty, he felt rivaled the Bois de Boulogne. He liked to walk, he had always liked walking, and led me eagerly over the busy Avenida Constituyentes, by way of the same footbridge on which earlier we'd stood talking about Candela, past the large hospital, Centro Hospitalario del Estado Mayor Presidencial, under the noisy autopista, then into the park itself, by the Children's Museum, from where, in a lazy, desultory fashion, we made our way along a tangle of lightly shaded paths to La Feria and Lago mayor, the largest of the park's three lakes, at the edge of which we sat for a spell beneath the old cedars to look at the paddle boats and ducks.

He'd long dreamt of writing a handbook for travelers to Mexico City, he told me, once we were settled there, one in the style of the old Baedeker's guides so popular in the days of Henry James. Recently he'd purchased a small, leather-bound edition of the same, Baedeker's 1897 vade mecum to Central Italy and Rome, which he'd chanced upon one day in an antiquarian bookshop in Bruges and had brought along to show me, drawing it out of his pack like a magician a rabbit from his hat. It was a beautiful, dusty-smelling book with lightly marbled end-pages and a number of colored fold-out maps and plans. He loved everything about it, the book—the binding, the typeface, even the editor's preface, the opening of which he insisted on reading aloud to me:

> The objects of the Handbook for Italy, which consists of three volumes, each complete in itself, are to supply the traveler with some information regarding the progress of civilization and art among the people he is about to visit, to render him as independent as possible of the services of guides and valets-de-place, to protect him against extortion, and in every way to aid him in deriving enjoyment and instruction from his tour in one of the most fascinating countries in the world. The Handbook will also, it is hoped, be the means of saving the traveler many a trial of temper; for there are few countries where the patience is more severely taxed than in some parts of Italy.

A trial of temper! He liked that phrase especially, for always it made him picture the stodgy young James, guidebook in hand, picking his way through the beggars in the Forum! Yet what he most admired about the preface, what he felt distinguished the guidebooks of then from the guidebooks of now, was the editor's assertion—a conviction really—that the object of travel (to any country, any place) consisted of nothing less than a thoroughgoing study of "the progress of civilization and art" as was to be found in that land. To know the Rome of Baedeker, Murray, and Hare was to walk its streets, to read its poets, to haunt its churches, to seek out, in corners dark and bright, its many time-worn statues, fountains, and shrines. To know Rome truly was to know its architecture, its politics and history, its gaudy patron saints. One must see the Pantheon, the Colosseum, and St. Peter's, of course, but the real Rome, the deeper Rome, lay elsewhere, he insisted to me, revealing itself only slowly, to those with the temperament, interest, and time. In a city like Rome one must be *taught* to see, to fathom the past at one's feet. "It is a place secret, sensuous, oblique, a poem and to be known as a poem," he quoted happily from a book about the same by the American writer Eleanor Clark, who, by coincidence, had loved Mexico City, too, where for a time she'd worked as a translator for the exiled Leon Trotsky.

"Look here," said Arsène, interrupting my thoughts about Trotsky (I'd once spent an afternoon in his garden in Coyoacán), selecting a page from the guidebook at random and running a finger down the page: "The Arch of Janus...the Cloaca Maxima...yes, here we go, the Church of Santa Maria in Cosmedin," he cried with delight, squinting over the top of his glasses to read the tiny print: "a church, a basilica, 'sometimes called Bocca della Verità from the ancient circular drain-head to the left in the portico, into the mouth of which, according to a medieval belief, the ancient Romans thrust their right hands when taking an oath.' The Mouth of Truth—right there on the portico! Why, one could walk right by it and never know. Do you get what I'm talking about? Do you see what I mean?"

To my relief, the question was merely rhetorical, for he didn't even look at me, but continued at once, as if in further illustration of his point, to describe for me the so-called "Porta Magica" of the Villa Palombaro there, on one wall of which one could find a series of ancient cabalistic characters containing a formula for making gold!

I knew that he and Simin had spent some time

in Rome after their daughter left for college. They'd even talked of moving there, of selling their apartment in Manhattan and making a life for themselves abroad. They'd been happy in Italy, at least relatively so, for they'd fought terribly, too, as Simin had been at pains to tell me that year, often calling me from the apartment of one of her Roman friends to share with me the latest about their bickering, the various curses and recriminations, and about her ongoing affair with a friend of ours, a dalliance, a liaison, for which she wasn't in the least bit sorry, she'd insisted each time, only a bit puzzled some nights when she remembered the little things Arsène had once said to her that had made her think she could live her whole life without longing, though she'd never believed it, not really. He'd never have promised such a thing.

THE FIRST TIME SIMIN had had sex with our friend David was on the roof of her building one summer night, after Arsène had been called away to the hospital, leaving the two of them alone with their drinks, their silence, which had seemed to quiver in the air between them. She'd never liked him, David, his dark, wiry hair, his patronizing way with facts, and over the years had let him know it in a host of subtle and not-so-subtle ways, so that she'd been surprised that night, when, rather than bidding her goodbye, he'd taken her husband's chair instead, then taken her hand to look at the ring she was wearing, a gaudy little ring her aunt had given her, which she'd slipped on her finger, a whim. Then his hand was up her skirt, it had happened that fast, she'd told me, so that she'd moaned despite herself, shifting her hips to accommodate him, his breath on her neck was hot. She'd told me that and more, when for a time I'd refused to take her calls, to speak with her at all.

Yet even those details (had she stopped there, with them) had been enough to incriminate me, to make me complicit in her affair. Understand, my objection was not a moral one: her life, her marriage, was her own. What troubled me then (what troubles me still) was her power to persuade me—even against the evidence of my eyes and ears. She'd done it before, she'd done it many times before, charging our relationship with an intimacy, a candor, I'd come to dread, though she'd never actually asked me for anything, not for alibis or favors, not even for my approval, my blessing. All she'd ever asked of me (though she'd never actually asked it) was that I allow her to speak. I could think what I liked of her; she'd said as much herself: I could hate her, I could pity her, my heart could seethe with contempt. It mattered little, as long as I listened, as long as I lent her my ear.

And so I had, so that over the years she'd filled my head with her stories, dark raging torrents, sometimes cold fickle streams of her words. She'd told me everything, she'd stopped at nothing—at it had cost me little, I was sure.

SHE COULDN'T BEAR TO be alone; that was the heart of it. For as long as I'd known Simin, she'd feared nothing so much as the thoughts in her own head. Only by speaking them aloud to someone, *anyone*, any pretense would do, could she breathe at peace again, could she feel at ease in her skin. It was a weakness, a liability in her, which to others seemed a virtue, a strength. The taxi driver, the waiter at lunch, the girl at the register where she stopped to buy flowers—they loved her for her warmth, her complaisance, for the faith and knowing in her eyes.

Whenever she traveled some place new the first thing she did was to get a measure of the people there, in the inn or hotel in which she was staying, and in the local shops and restaurants, so as to familiarize herself with the various men and women on whom—for reasons she could never predict—she might be forced to rely, to *depend*, chatting freely with the landlady, the clerk behind the desk, even with the local mechanics, whom she'd greeted where she'd found them behind the shop one morning, smoking glumly in the sun.

Her car had broken down while I was staying with her in the south of France one summer, where she'd rented a house in the old Languedoc town of Uzès, so that instead of hiking the hills near the Pont du Gard, as we'd planned, we'd spent the morning sitting on the curb in front of the local repair shop, chatting blithely with the other customers, and with the mechanics themselves, in particular with a young man named Jean-Louis, a specialist in German cars, who'd been much taken with my friend, with her long pale legs, and with her eyes, which, when she smiled at one, turned the strangest shade of green.

I remember she'd told him about the book she was writing on ioculares or joglars, the popular entertainers of Provence who'd given rise, by the end of the eleventh century, to the poets known as troubadours. How much he'd followed of what she'd said had been difficult to tell, though he'd smiled and nodded and studied her large, mobile mouth with an intensity that had made me think he was reading her lips.

If Simin was eloquent in English, she was bewitching in French, so that it wasn't long before a small crowd had gathered around us where we'd sat on the curb before the shop, smiling and laughing and generally enjoying her brashness, her wit. That *she'd* needed *them* that morning would have surprised them to learn, that the beautiful, cocksure woman needed anyone at all.

Yet that was her method, her trick: the more gregariously she behaved, the more miserable, more wretched she felt. I'd seen it before, many times, that other flagrant self. For she'd been moody all morning, and impatient with me, though I'd scarcely said a thing. When pressed over dinner at a restaurant that evening, she'd confessed that our friend David had just left her after a glorious week in bed, that he'd returned to New York, to his wife and children, and that his absence made her hateful and sick.

Of course, the feeling would pass, she'd chuckled sourly, draining the last of her wine. They weren't *actually* in love. It was the intimacy she missed, that instant corroboration of everything she yearned for, of everything she knew. To dream alone was too much for her; she hated it, she'd told me—the laughter, the music, the ringing in her ears. And she'd hated the people at the table beside us that evening, with their smug little faces, with their mouths that never stopped chewing.

To that and more I'd listened with patience where we sat there in the bustling Place aux Herbes, though

I'd heard it all before, at different times, in different forms, so that as she'd talked I'd been able to focus on her features instead: her high pale forehead, her aquiline nose, and her lips—so wry, so slender—which I'd often thought to kiss.

ARSÈNE HIMSELF HAD BEEN charmed by her mouth; it was one of the first things he'd noticed about her the day I introduced them in Washington Square Park. Seated together on a bench near the arch, Simin had been in the midst of telling me a story about a recently married woman she knew who'd disappeared from her house one day only to reappear at the kitchen table, some six months later, where her husband found her reading the paper and eating a hard-boiled egg!

I remember the way Arsène had looked at her that day, as though he were struggling to focus his eyes, to make sense of what they knew. He'd smirked; I remember that; he'd laughed a little. And I remember him shaking his head. Even when he himself was talking (he'd just read the novel *Washington Square* and was eager to talk about it), he'd studied her mouth as if not quite willing or *able* to believe.

It had happened to be a novel Simin loved, one she'd read many times, so that they'd spoken at length about the story that day, about the sweet if vapid Catherine, and about her stern and cynical father, Dr. Sloper. Simin had quoted lines from the novel by heart, about the doctor: "...there was nothing abstract in his remedies—he always ordered you to take something", about his daughter's faithless suitor, Mr. Townsend: "...for, after all, Morris was very unwilling to be the cause of her being disinherited", and about Catherine herself, poor Catherine and her cream cakes, citing with delight: "...though it is an awkward confession to make about one's heroine, I must add she was something of a glutton"!

That evening in Uzès, I'd remembered it all—the park, the pigeons, the ease with which the three of us had talked that day. Naturally, we'd changed since then; *she'd* changed: her fine, black hair was shorter, she'd painted her nails, she was quicker to laugh at herself, a dry, still, unhappy laugh. Yet her face and figure were the same, or if not the same then nearly so.

I remember she'd looked beautiful where we'd sat there by the fountain beneath a netting of fine white lights—her avid hands, her subtle, high-arched feet (she'd kicked off her sandals), and her breasts, naked beneath her t-shirt (which I'd seen that afternoon, which I'd seen all my life), her small, pouty breasts with their large, dark nipples, to which she'd never given a thought when dressing in my presence or when sunbathing on the wide stone terrace of her little rented house there, where we'd often spent the afternoons reading, drinking wine, and reminiscing about our lives, though mostly I'd just listened, sometimes closing my eyes to think.

Occasionally when she was feeling restless she'd taken me into town with her to buy wine and postcards or just to wander the empty, sunbaked streets. She'd rented a bright red Citroën in which some days we'd charged around the arid countryside, picking wildflowers and stopping for wine or pastis in one of the many roadside cafés. She'd rarely mentioned her work, ostensibly the reason she was there. In fact, I never saw her open a book but to close it at once. Nor did she type or make notes, at least not in my presence, though she filled the days there with words, speaking rashly, madly at times, as if charting the dimensions of some dark, capacious space.

Yet about certain things she'd been conspicuously silent. She'd said nothing or little about the food we'd eaten, mostly olives, cheese, and bread, or about the lumpy old beds on which we'd slept, let alone about the town itself, with its ducal castle, its narrow, cobbled streets, and its soaring campanile, the ancient

Tour Fenestrelle. What's more, she'd scarcely said a word about Arsène but to disparage him, and always in ways—petty ways—that had made me think she was trying to get a rise out of me, to goad me, pressing me, *tempting* me to accuse her, to defend him, to speak as a friend in his stead. If one day she mocked him for his effusiveness, his chatter, the next day she rebuked him for his indifference, his sloth.

Yet it was of his pedantry—his books and papers, the sheer presumption of it all—that she was particularly critical. A scholar herself, she'd come to detest his restless erudition, the way it distracted him, drawing him inward, away from her, as he spoke, so that what at first she'd found so impressive in him, his raptness, his abstraction, his sometimes breathless volubility, had become the very source of her resentment, her rage. There on her wide stone terrace in France, she'd warned me to be wary of him, that he was not the man he seemed.

CERTAINLY, ARSÈNE KNEW NONE of that where we sat by the lake that day. He was eating a popular flavor of ice cream called tres leches with a small wooden spoon, two scoops of which he'd purchased from one of the many strolling vendors there. He could be happy that way, deeply, simply content. Indeed, there was something of the child about him in the pleasure he found in everyday things—in food and drink, in birds and flowers, in the particular fit of a new pair of shoes.

He was telling me about his plan—long anticipated—to retire here in Mexico City. Now that his daughter was married, now that she was secure in her profession, he felt it was time for a change.

His plan was simple: if all went well, he would sell his apartment in New York and live here, in Condesa, where each day he would rise early, walk for a couple of hours, then return to his apartment to write.

Yet it was the simple prospect of reading—every night, every day—to which he most looked forward. For years he'd been making lists of the books he hoped to read or *re*read, the titles of which he'd filed away in cupboards and cabinets and drawers. Some days he did nothing but think about books.

In addition to the volume on Candela (which he'd read once, in a flurry, and now was reading again, with more patience, more care), *Black Lamb and Grey Falcon* by Rebecca West, Ford Madox Ford's *The Good Soldier*, an introduction to "human geography" called *Space and Place* by an American geographer named Yi-Fu Tuan, *The Grammar of North Indian Ragas* by Bimalakanta

Roychaudhuri, Gustaf Sobin's *Luminous Debris*, and the notebooks of Simone Weil, he was working his way through a well-known study by Foucault, one he'd started in French some months ago, while in Paris, then left on a plane, only to take up again, in English, in New York, a history of madness called *Folie et Déraison: Histoire de la folie à l'âge classique* or *Madness and Civilization: A History of Insanity in the Age of Reason.*

Having initially lost the book, only to find himself still thinking about Foucault, he'd taken up the author's equally well-known study, *Les Mots et les choses* or *The Order of Things*, a used paperback edition of which he'd happened to have at hand among his books in New York, and which he couldn't help thinking about now, he told me, licking the ice cream from his lips, even as he was reading and thinking about Foucault's *Madness and Civilization*, a new clothbound copy of which he'd purchased shortly after he'd lost his paperback original, so that in his mind the ideas from the one book had gotten muddled with the ideas from the other, the result of which (a result that clearly pleased him) was that, though he'd intended to share with me his thoughts about *Madness and Civilization*, which he'd jotted down in a small black notebook he kept in his pack, he spoke instead about Foucault's *The Order of Things*, only the preface and first two chapters of which he'd managed to read by then, the mere thought of which pages so moved him where we sat by the lake that day that more than once he all but sprang to his feet.

That, *that exactly*, was what he loved most about reading Foucault, he told me that morning, the fact that even a single page of his work (no matter the subject, the book) was enough to thrill him for days. To read Foucault, any Foucault, was to be startled, amazed, to find your world turned inside-out. It was a feeling Foucault himself had known well, Arsène insisted to me that day, only to recount for me one such experience, one such aperçu, which he, Foucault, describes at length in his preface to *The Order of Things*, an encounter he'd had with a particular passage by Borges in which the Argentine fabulist tells the story of a certain taxonomy included in a "certain Chinese encyclopedia" in which the divisions between animals ("a. belonging to the Emperor, b. embalmed, c. tame, d. sucking pigs. e. sirens…"), had made him laugh out loud where he'd sat reading in his study one night, shattering the "familiar landmarks" of his thought by "breaking up all the ordered surfaces and all the planes with which we are accustomed to tame the wild profusion of existing things."

Such was the way Arsène had talked that day, as if he were running out of breath or as if he were trying to catch his breath, having been winded by a fall from some high, unwholesome place. Yet such behavior was hardly new; indeed, in his affect he seemed very much the same to me, if perhaps a little more so, for there were moments (I remember them now) when he stiffened beside me, cocking his head as if suddenly alert to himself, to his lips, his tongue, to the avid, anxious beating of his heart. More than once I felt he was watching himself through my eyes.

And there were times, who knows how many, when suddenly he stopped what he was saying to look at me, and I was certain he'd confront me at last.

STANDING NOW AT THE window of his apartment in Condesa, I consider the busy avenue below, with its taxis and motorbikes, its milling crowds, its wide, ragged median of dark-smelling trees, and try to recover the particular feeling of that day—the clouds, the people, the dankness of the air, try to see him, my friend, as I saw him then, as he'd led me through the park, try to recast him in the present, where he belongs, where he was happiest, I know. I try to conjure his voice, the tilt of his head, the way he squeezed my arm as we walked, try to hear again what he was telling me that day, what for years he'd been trying to say.

It was his sister, Péroline, who'd told me he was dead. She'd called me from Paris one day, shortly after I'd returned to New York, briefly identifying herself before dispatching me posthaste, back here to Mexico City, to dispose of his things. The body? She'd taken care of it, she'd assured me brusquely. Only his apartment was my concern.

Of course, she would pay me for my time, she'd added in French. All she'd required was that I get here at once, without delay, and that I keep the details (whatever they were) to myself. I could do what I liked with his books.

Positioned two flights above a restaurant called *Cortes al Carbón*, in a drab, salmon-colored building at the intersection of Calle Campeche and Avenida Michoacán, the apartment consists of a clean, modern-looking kitchen (rarely used), a bathroom with double sinks, two small bedrooms with built-in closets, and a narrow, prow-shaped living room that makes me feel, where I'm standing at the window now, like I'm cutting through the streets of the city on a sleek and sea-bound ship. Only sparsely furnished, the place is filled with the sounds of spring traffic—the honking of cars and trucks, the wailing of sirens, the hum of music and voices from the restaurant below.

I'm not sure what initially surprised me about the place, that is, beyond the fact that he'd never invited me to see it, not once. In fact, there was nothing unusual about it, at least that I could see. With its coffered ceilings and creaking hardwood floors, it seemed like every other apartment I've known. The windows stuck, the faucets leaked, a few of the tiles in the bathroom were missing. While I'd often been a guest in his apartment in New York, a gloomy old walk-up by the river, he'd rarely ever mentioned this place to me, always refusing my offer to see him home, after a day spent walking, though my apartment, the one I rent, is just a few blocks away.

What surprised me about the place was just that: that he was not a private man. He'd never been so. Like Simin, if for different reasons, he'd liked to think aloud, so that over the years he'd made me privy to the widest conceivable range of his impressions. As with those traditional Japanese houses, so designed as to blur the distinction between inside and out, he'd spoken to me with a frankness and sincerity that had often made me think his thoughts and feelings were my own.

GETTING INTO HIS APARTMENT had not been easy. It had taken me a few days to finally reach his landlady, who'd been away visiting friends in Chilpancingo, so that I'd passed the time, in the semi-furnished apartment I rent here by corresponding with a woman, an archivist at Princeton University, who is helping me to track down some letters I need for a talk I'm scheduled to give in New York next month on the late Mexican diplomat and writer Sergio Pitol, letters he'd written to his friends and fellow writers, Witold Gombrowicz, Rosario Castellanos, and Elena Poniatowska.

His landlady had been friendly enough when I rang the doorbell yesterday, ushering me into a small, dark office beneath the stairs, where she'd offered me a can of iced coffee to drink. The air conditioner in the window was broken; she'd turned the switch to show me, before settling herself on the plump green sofa by the desk, from where she'd considered me with a flushed and anxious look. Her father had died the week before, she'd told me, as if to explain herself, and then *this*, she'd added, gesturing vaguely over her head, in the direction of what I assumed to be the apartment she'd rented to my friend. Now the *business* was hers, she'd said without feeling, by which term she might have meant the business of the office in which we'd sat (with its copier and fax machine and large potted plants) or else the business of Arsène, of his sad, untimely death. She'd told me this, when for a spell we'd sat without talking. We'd smiled; we'd sipped our coffees; she'd adjusted her blouse. At length, after securing a set of keys from a drawer in the desk, she'd led me back out into the lobby, then up the tiled stairs.

She'd told me that her sister had wanted her to hire a priest to "clear the air" in the apartment before she rented it again, but she'd refused the suggestion, having never really liked her sister, having never liked her sister's priest, a bibulous old man with terrible small teeth. In any case the air had seemed fine to her, if perhaps a little stuffy, she'd remarked to me, as I'd followed her into the apartment. After all, it wasn't as if my friend had been murdered here. He'd simply been unhappy— and where was the crime in that?

It was from an old gas pipe that Arsène had hung himself. In the cool, hollow-sounding bathroom she'd showed me the painted pipe, indicating, with a twist of her hand, the way he'd looped the cord around it, then pulled it tight. It was she who'd found him there.

She was curious about the book he was writing on the empress, she'd told me, by the way, perhaps hoping that I, his friend, would elaborate on the matter for her. Apparently, they'd talked about the project in some detail, for she'd had a host of questions about Carlota, smart, specific questions about her sexuality, her madness, and about her fateful meeting with Napoleon III, only a few of which I'd been able to answer to her satisfaction, having only ever seen a few rough chapters of the book. She'd had some theories, too: that Maximilian was a homosexual; that he was impotent, his penis misshapen; that it was he himself, with the help of his Indian lover, who'd poisoned his wife and driven her mad.

She'd told me that, when she'd showed me the latest draft of his book, where he'd left it in a drawer. Certainly, she was familiar with his things, opening the cabinets, replacing his CDs in the rack, and pouring me a glass of water from the large plastic tank by the stove. Only when she'd received a call on her cell phone had she left me alone.

TIRED NOW, I CONSIDER THE ROOM. It was here that Arsène had done most of his living. Against one wall he'd arranged a small desk, three tall bookshelves, and a pair of old filing cabinets, the kind once found in banks. In the center of the room is a large sisal rug. The only other furniture in the room is a standing lamp and a cracked leather armchair in which (so his landlady told me) he'd liked to sit by the window and think. On the wall by the door he'd tacked a large map of Mexico City, the *Guía Roji*, 2013.

His desk is just as he'd left it. By his laptop is a legal pad, a container of pens and pencils, and a variety of books, including two volumes of poetry in French (neither of which is familiar to me); Piglia's *The Diaries of Emilio Renzi: The Happy Years*; the novel *Noticias del Imperio* by Fernando del Paso; a hardcover copy (uninscribed) of one of his mother's earliest studies, *Twisted Love: Jewish Women and the Third Reich*; a yellowed paperback edition of *Othello* (Biblioteca Basica Salvat); *Trieste* by Daša Drndić; *The Empress of Farewells* by Prince Michael of Greece; a dog-eared copy of *Foucault's The Order of Things* (with bookmark from Saint George's English Bookstore, Berlin); and the seventh volume of the *Encyclopedia Judaica*, apparently the only one from the set. On his chair itself, as if just set there, is a stack of psychiatric journals, mostly from the U.S. and France.

Above his desk, on the cracked plaster wall, is a picture of the bold young empress in black lace staring defiantly at the photographer; a blank airmail envelope from the Royal Hotel in Bangkok (held in place by a piece of cellophane tape); a snapshot of his daughter as a child by the sea; and a lithograph (cut from a magazine or book) of Bouchout Castle in Belgium, where, following the execution of Maximilian by the revolutionary forces of Benito Juárez, the empress had died of her grief.

I'd arrived here this morning, determined to dispatch with his effects as swiftly and efficiently as possible. Apart from a few reminders for Élise, which I'd take back to New York with me, I'd planned to dispose of the rest, even his books, packing them into boxes and hiring someone—anyone—to haul them away.

Yet it is evening now and I've hardly touched a thing. I've smoked, I've gazed out the window, and I've read a bit, whatever has caught my eye: a poem by Whitman, an article on fornix-region deep brain stimulation from *The New England Journal of Medicine*, and the first brief chapter of *The Origins of Totalitarianism*, a bloated, water-stained copy of which I found by the toilet when I went to the bathroom to piss.

As surprised as I'd been to receive the phone call from his sister, the news of his death had come as a relief to me, even as it had sickened me, so that I can barely recall what else she'd said to me that day. There were candlesticks; I remember that. And there was a small painting (a tree in a field, I think) that she'd asked me to find. As a courtesy, I'd considered telling her something about her brother, from whom she'd long been estranged, something about his work, his depression, about our walk in Chapultepec Park, but she'd seemed impatient with me, speaking quickly, peremptorily, before hanging up the phone.

IT WAS WHILE I was sitting in the park with Arsène that day that he told me the story (I'd never actually heard it before) of how Simin had broken her leg in Amsterdam one night. Merely mentioning her injury, and the months they'd spent together in Holland, was enough to quicken in me a host of dark, ungainly feelings, where I sat beside there him, not one of which I was able to settle, to manage in my head, so that at first I merely goggled at him.

It had started simply enough: feeling peevish, he'd dared Simin to jump across a narrow drainage channel that ran along one side of the street on which they'd been walking, somewhere near the Waterloopleinmarkt. He should have known better, for they'd been drinking and the street was slick with rain, but he'd been unable to resist the temptation (as it turned out, the very point of his story), pressing her hard until, with a flutter of her coat, she'd jumped.

It was his motive that puzzled him. He couldn't remember having been angry with her; surely, he would never have *tried* to hurt her. It simply didn't make sense, for they'd just spent a lovely day together, browsing the local bookshops, eating pastries, and wandering through the dank-smelling rooms of the Rijksmuseum, in one of which she'd fallen in love with a painting of a windmill on a polder by an artist named Gabriël.

That he remembered clearly, the way she'd grinned and squinted at the tiny Hague School painting. He remembered the rain, the dampness of his socks, and the strange, mineral scent of her skin. And he remembered the shawl she'd been wearing, a fine Kashmiri stole, which she'd received as a gift from a friend. He practically bubbled with the facts of that day: her jade earrings, her particular shade of lipstick, the spot of lipstick on her fine white teeth. She'd broken the heel of one of her shoes while they were walking, so that she'd been forced to buy an expensive and impractical pair in a tiny shop in the Jordaan where the saleswoman—hardly more than girl—had sniffed at them where they'd stood dripping with rain, a recollection that lit up his eyes and made him smile. For everything they'd done that day had seemed charmed to him, each incident, each encounter, a part of some greater, more luminous whole.

Simin had accepted a fellowship to teach for a semester at the university in Leiden that year, exchanging their apartment for the home of a fellow professor in Amstelveen. It had seemed the very change they'd needed. Refreshed, bewildered, they'd gorged themselves on herring, stamppotten, and rijsttafels, and each day they'd marveled like newlyweds at their tidy little house tucked snugly between identical brick houses just across the street from what remained of a putrid old canal.

Then suddenly Simin had grown impatient with him, clicking her tongue, scraping her chair at the table, and generally drinking too much, too much gin, which had made her fractious and grim. He'd seen the change in her before, that queer retreat inward, which, as ever, he'd been helpless to avert, to explain, so that in the weeks and months that followed he'd kept largely to himself, reading late at night, sleeping in the den, and taking the train into Amsterdam each morning, where he'd wandered without purpose in the rain.

Yet he didn't regret their time there, not at all, he told me. While Simin had long been a mystery to him (for years he'd mistaken the quality for love itself), he felt he'd come to a different, more flexuous understanding of her in the dark winter months they'd lived in Amstelveen. He'd seen things in her he'd never seen before, strange, sometimes beautiful things that had made him wonder if he'd really ever known her at all.

SIMIN'S FATHER HAD DIED that year they were living in Holland. A heart attack. Her sister had telephoned her from New York one evening, her mother too tired, too angry, to speak.

"Yes, yes...when?" Simin had said.

The news had not surprised her, though she'd loved her father dearly, having never been close to him, their love but an invention of hers, something she'd dreamt as a girl in her head.

He, like her mother, had been born in Tehran. They'd met as professors there, had fallen in love, then gotten married. Then there'd been a scandal of sorts, one involving her mother, something *sexual*, suspected Simin, though she'd never managed to confirm it.

Not even the rush and roar of New York had been enough to draw her father out of his study after that; the life he'd built for himself in their apartment in Tehran he'd merely replicated in their apartment on Riverside Drive, so that, growing up, Simin had rarely seen the man but in passing, when occasionally he'd emerged from the bathroom with a towel around his neck or when, with briefcase in hand, he'd trundled his way out the door. He'd seemed to live inside his head, she'd told me, a place she could scarcely imagine but as a paradise of flowers and birds.

Her best memories of him were from their summers together in France, in Lyon, where as a young man he'd studied archeology, and to which city they'd returned as a family each June, so that her father could confer with his friends and colleagues there, which had mostly meant talking and drinking wine and searching the arid hillsides of Provence and Languedoc for potsherds and coins or the remains of some ancient Roman mill.

His specialty was the Achaemenid Empire. While living and teaching in Iran, he'd spent decades studying the ruins of Pasargadae, near Shiraz, the ancient Persian capital of Cyrus the Great. It was just as he'd begun work in helping to excavate the great pot-hoard soon to be known as the Pasargadae Treasure that the scandal had broken and his wife had been forced to resign.

Simin believed it was that—even more than his wife's infidelity—that had ruined him, that had shattered his spirit. It was a job that would have made him his name.

She'd told me that one evening in Riverside Park, where we'd gone for our usual walk. From there, we could see the lights of New Jersey, a dull, sulphurous glow that had always made me think of the chemical plants and oil refineries clustered like mushrooms on the vast, marshy wastelands to the south. Whenever Arsène worked late she and I would walk and talk that way, often ending the night in some bar or restaurant on Broadway, where to amuse me, perhaps to reward me for my friendship, my patience, she would tell me the most outlandish, most prosaic of things.

There by the river one night she told me everything she knew about her father—that he'd never loved his parents, that he'd fathered a son out of wedlock in France, that, just as they were making their plans to leave Tehran, he'd been detained for three days by the secret police.

Of course, he himself had never told her any of that. It was from her mother, and from her aunt, her mother's sister, Esfir, that she'd learned the little she knew about her father, details with which, over time, she'd made herself a man she could fathom, could see.

I'd met her father many times, while she and I were in college together. Whenever she'd grown tired of the food in the dining hall, she'd invited me to the family apartment, overlooking the river, where we'd eaten dinner with her mother, her elegant mother, at the long mahogany table, from one end of which she'd laughed and teased us and smoked her *Gitanes*. She'd assumed we were lovers, that we were carrying on in secret, no matter how hotly we'd protested it, no matter how chastely we'd behaved. I'd always liked her, Simin's mother, her poise, her beauty, on the surface of which I'd sometimes imagined the finest, most subtle of cracks.

Simin's father had rarely joined us for dinner when I was there. Most nights, he'd eaten alone in his study, the depths of which I'd occasionally caught a glimpse when he slipped out to use the bathroom or when he was teaching an evening class. The room was filled to bursting with books, Arsène had been pleased to tell me, following his first long evening in their home. Her father, perhaps tipsy from the wine he'd served them at dinner that night, perhaps flattered by the attention of such a bright, inquisitive young man, perhaps merely taken by the chance to discourse at length in French, had invited Arsène, after dinner, to sit in the chair by his desk, from which, in the dim, low-cast light, Arsène had been able to examine the cramped, exotic space: the books, the carpets, the paintings, as well as the various relics Simin's father had brought with him from Iran, a dusty hodgepodge of oil lamps, potsherds, stamp seals, and coins.

They'd talked well into the night on that occasion, drinking and laughing and generally reminiscing about France, a country for which Arsène himself had never felt the absence to miss.

Yet they'd never spoken again, not really. When next Arsène had seen Simin's father in their apartment, the man had seemed not to recognize him, nodding his head at him as one might at a delivery boy or at a plumber come to fix the kitchen sink. On only one other occasion, in the yard on Long Island where their wedding was held, had her father addressed Arsène by name, though by then he'd had nothing to say.

In Holland, Arsène had spent much of his time exploring the neighborhoods of Amsterdam, in particular those near the Eastern Docklands, like Oostenberg, Czaar Peterbuurdt, Het Funen, and Zeeburg, and later those to the south and west, venturing further and further out each day to the distant edges of the city, so that by the time he'd returned to Amstelveen each evening he'd been nearly dead on his feet.

He'd just begun to feel restless there, he told me, when our friend David had paid them a visit from New York. It had fallen to Arsène to entertain him during the day, while Simin was at work, a charge with which he couldn't have been happier, so that together they'd visited the popular sights: the parks and markets and museums. One day they'd taken a bus to see the windmills of Kinderdijk. It was there that David had told him about the Hague School painters, information Arsène had later shared with Simin, when they'd toured the galleries at the Rijksmuseum.

As they'd strolled between the windmills that day, David had spoken to him of the painters, Bilders, Bosboom, and Maris, and of the woeful outsider, Jozef Israëls. David's father, also a painter, had loved their work, their devotion to the dreary Dutch landscape, to its wan, anemic light. For two weeks, when David was ten, he and his father had wandered the beaches and polders near Den Haag, his father taking photographs and making sketches, from which each evening he'd filled tablet after tablet of watercolor pages. It had rained most of the time they were there, the sea too cold for swimming, so that all David remembered of his father's many paintings were their endless shades of gray.

Many of the tensions Arsène had felt with Simin while they were living there in Holland had seemed to vanish in David's presence, so that they'd spent their evenings together, as the rain poured down outside, with a calm and satisfaction they hadn't known in years.

David was smart and funny and spoke some nights about his failing marriage with an irony, a pathos, that had made him glow with a warm and gentle light. He was arrogant, he had always been arrogant, though always with a willingness to lay himself bare. He was good at things, many things, and not so good at others, each of which he was happy to retail for them. He was miserable at marriage and sports; he was helpless with money and tools. If something broke in his apartment he promptly hired someone to fix it. He didn't care what had happened to it. Such was his impatience that he didn't want to know.

Simin herself had seemed younger, livelier for his company, tying back her hair at night, laughing easily, and wearing perfume. She'd sung and danced; for their entertainment she'd recited Breton, Villon, and Rimbaud.

While David was their guest, Arsène had shared a bed with Simin again, a large old bed at the head of the stairs. It had been months since they'd had sex, he'd lost track of the time, so that he'd been surprised one night when, after an evening of drinking and dancing with David, she'd reached for his penis in bed.

She'd trimmed her pubic hair; it was something he remembered, something she'd never done before, a remark for which he apologized to me at once, fearing it had cheapened his meaning. He'd only mentioned it because it had struck him as strange.

David had stayed with them for another week, before taking the train to Berlin one morning to confer with some colleagues in the field. At first Simin had seemed unfazed by his departure, joking and laughing and tying back her hair. David had left them some hash, which they'd smoked before the fire one night, but it had given her a headache, so that after watching a little television she'd retreated alone to her bed.

Some nights later Arsène had thought he'd heard her crying.

OVER THE YEARS, I'D often thought of telling him about Simin, about her affair, about her hatred and mockery of him. In fact I *had* told him, many times—though perhaps in ways too cryptic, too errant to grasp. In my sympathy, my pity for him, I'd even considered taking him for a walk one day and leading him past some restaurant or café in which I knew Simin and David were meeting, so that he could discover them himself.

Yet it wouldn't have worked: I'm sure of it. For even if he'd found them there, heads bent over glasses of wine, he'd never have suspected a thing, not Arsène, but would have hailed them from the street, perhaps even leaned over the planter, if they were eating outside, to remark upon the food on their plates.

He wasn't oblivious; far from it. In matters dear to him he could be keenly discriminating. Ask him anything about orchids or furniture or antique Turkish rugs, and he might never stop talking. He was one of those men who saw the world largely as he liked to, as he wished it to be. What's more he trusted Simin. He'd never had a reason not to.

STILL SHAKEN BY HIS story, and uncertain what to say, I asked him about his mother, about her death last winter, a question to which, for a spell, he could only shake his head. She'd only just returned to Cleveland, after a month of living with her sister in Florida, he told me, clearly perplexed. She'd been happy there, swimming, eating shrimp, and collecting shells on the narrow strip of beach below the bridge behind her sister's house, some of which he'd found in a plastic bag by her bed. So why had she returned?

That winter had been a particularly cold one on Lake Erie, a dark, brittle season during which his mother had scarcely left her apartment but to check her mailbox in the lobby. She'd been drinking again, he explained, drinking and taking pills for the pain in her legs, so that for weeks she'd eaten almost nothing. When he'd found her, she was lying naked beneath a sheet on the floor. The television was on, some anchorman screaming.

He said this to me, when for a time we sat without talking. Only when he seemed to have recovered himself did he tell me about the fear he felt, now that she was dead. It was a fear he'd felt before, some years ago, when his only uncle had died.

He'd never really known the man, his mother's only sibling, though as a child he'd looked forward to his yearly visit to Paris, to the gifts he brought with him, and to their usual walk to a nearby park, where on a bench made small by a large, dry fountain his uncle would tell him about Japan.

"It was there in Japan, in the northern port city of Aomori, that my uncle died alone one evening," explained Arsène. "As a collector of fine porcelain, he'd traveled there by train one day to meet with a dealer about acquiring a certain rare pagoda teapot, which meeting and teapot he'd described in detail in the thick, leather-bound journal he'd kept of his travels there. The journal, written partly in English, partly in Japanese (at least annotated with what appeared to be Japanese characters), was essentially a catalogue, a register of names and places, of prices, dimensions, and dates. I remember being struck by the variety of pieces he'd examined in his travels throughout the country, each of which he'd noted for future reference in strange, often delightfully quotidian terms: 'barber's bowl', 'reticulated koro', 'imari sleeve vase', 'moon flask', and 'dutch decorated apothecary jar', to name the ones I recall.

"Having concluded his business in Aomori, he'd planned to take the ferry to the nearby island of Hokkaido the next day, on which island, in the modest resort town of Noboribetsu, he'd arranged to meet a Japanese woman with whom he'd fallen in love. He was standing at the window of his hotel room that evening, sipping a beer and gazing out at the rainy harbor and 'white-flecked sea' (his journal had ended with these details), when he'd suffered a heart attack and collapsed on the floor.

"It was less than six months later that I'd found myself standing in the self-same hotel," said Arsène, "in the very room in which my uncle had died, patiently awaiting my passage to Hokkaido the next day. In my attention to detail I was sipping a beer. I remember the wind and the rain, and I remember the book I was reading that evening—Quignard's *La haine de la musique*, which I'd learned about one evening from a lawyer in

Brest. I remember I'd drawn back the curtain over the window to consider the stormy harbor below, but had been unable to make out anything more than a shifting jumble of colors and shapes, as I'd left my glasses on the train. I remember cursing myself for my forgetfulness, while thinking about my uncle, who'd also been forgetful, and about the dinner I'd just eaten (a fried patty of minced squid with a bowl of sea urchin soup), which— the very same meal—my uncle had eaten, too.

"You see, at some point in the course of his travels in Japan, my uncle had fallen in love with a woman named Yume (he'd purchased a gift for her, a Meiji-era incense burner, which I'd seen for myself in a box of his things), so that as I'd stood there at the hotel window that evening, gazing down at the rain-swept harbor, at the shifting jumble of colors and shapes, I too had thought of her with longing, whoever she was, had pictured her watching television by herself in some well-kept room by the sea, unaware of what had happened to my uncle, the kindly old Frenchman she'd met.

"In my vision of her she was not thinking about my uncle, but was watching a popular comedy, a program she'd seen before, that made her feel restless where she sat there by the sea, so that she clenched her small fists and sighed." With that he paused for a moment, as if struggling to decipher the notion, when softly he added, "I spent only a single day on Hokkaido. Upon the recommendation of a guest in the ryokan in which I was staying, I ate a bowl of butter corn ramen at the restaurant next door, then spent an hour or so at a local hot spring, lost in my thoughts in the steam. Sadly, I never found her, Yume; I never even learned her last name."

A strange look crossed his face, when softly, uncertainly, he remarked, "Perhaps it's that, the lack of completion, that still troubles me. Things like that have always troubled me—idle, unfinished things. Ever since I was young, I've believed my life would add up to something, it must. Every time I've read a book, every time I've listened to a piece of music, every time I've travelled to some place new, I've done so knowing that it would be added to my tally, my sum, that one day my living would *tell*. Everything I've done and felt, I've done and felt with the understanding that it counted, it *mattered*—to someone somewhere somehow. It never occurred to me that a life might be for naught."

I REMEMBER FEELING RESTLESS, where we sat there that morning, and was about to suggest that we walk some more, that we take the opportunity to stretch our legs, when he asked me if I'd seen Simin lately. It was a question that caught me off guard, for just then I was thinking about her, about the last time we'd spoken, when she'd cursed me on the phone.

I'd just gotten home from work and was removing my shoes and socks, which had gotten soaked with rain, when my cell phone had buzzed. I'd decided not to answer it; I had nothing to say to Simin, and had actually started for the kitchen to fix myself a drink, when I'd picked up the phone.

She'd been crying, it was clear. That morning she'd received an email from her daughter, Élise, bitterly reproaching her for her affair with David, which Élise had learned about shortly after her wedding, a discovery that had all but ruined her honeymoon in Spain. Simin had blamed Arsène for it; she was certain it was he who'd told Élise as a way of getting even with her, as a way of making her pay. "The bastard!" she'd raged. "Is it my fault I didn't love him anymore, that I hadn't loved him for years? And what about Élise? The things she said! Good God! Should I have just *pretended* all that time? Would that have made her happy? Should I have settled for a life without love?"

To all of that I'd said nothing, or little. I'd known better than to speak to her when she was feeling wronged. Instead I'd let her talk, let her wear herself out.

Then for a few moments she'd fallen silent. I'd heard her light a cigarette, then exhale, when with a bitter chuckle she'd said,

"You don't think he told her, do you?"

"I don't know, Simin. I really don't know."

"But it doesn't seem like him, does it?"

"No. It doesn't seem like him."

"No? Well then fuck you!" she'd said. "It's clear you don't know him at all."

IT WAS TRUE. SITTING there beside him in the park that day, I hardly recognized him. It was shocking to admit, to recognize the fact that, for all the years we'd been friends, for all the times we'd shared, he remained a mystery to me, but a few quick lines, a sketch. At some point—who knows how long ago—I'd stopped seeing him, stopped hearing what he said. At some stage I'd simply settled for a version of him that suited me, one that in all likelihood bore little resemblance to the man he'd become, so that as he talked that morning I studied him with a rapt and abstract horror: his face, his hands, the curious way he sniffled when he spoke. His watch was new; at least I'd never seen it before. And his tooth, that crooked front tooth, had it always been that way? I didn't know, I couldn't say, when suddenly everything about him seemed strange. His lips moved, he squinted, he might have flapped his arms and flown off through the trees, for the little I knew of him.

Of course, I myself was to blame. The instant I'd answered Simin's call that night, the night she'd had sex with David, I'd set the whole ugly process in motion. I recall it distinctly, the sudden, dreadful feeling I'd had, as I'd listened to her talking, that a rift had opened up around me, that already, and for all I might regret it, my relationship with Arsène had changed. I couldn't have described it then, I can barely describe it now, the sense that the terms between us would never be the same.

Surely it was some time that night that Arsène had stopped stirring in my mind. At some point, as I'd listened to Simin, he'd ceased to exist for me, as he had, to speak, to suffer, to breathe. Even later that night, when I'd hung up the phone, when lying in bed I'd thought of Simin, of her ring, her panties, of David's breath on her neck, I'd felt no anger for her, strangely, let alone for David, whom I should have despised, but only for Arsène himself, for the fact that he'd trusted them there, on the rooftop alone, when he should have known better. The cuckold! The fool! Long before he left for the hospital that night, he should have sensed it in the air, that his wife was restless, uneasy, that his wife was *aroused*. He should have marked the transformation in her, should have recognized that her voice, her laughter, was different, that her very scent had changed. He should have noticed the signs—the giddiness, the fidgeting, the flush and moistness of her skin. He should have felt it in his bones the very instant his good friend David slipped a finger beneath the elastic of Simin's new panties then wrenched them to her knees.

The more I'd heard from her that night, the more I'd hated him, Arsène. I hadn't thought about it, really, I hadn't asked myself why. I remember it clearly. I was sitting stiffly at my desk, sitting stiffly in my chair. It was late, Simin was talking, I heard the traffic on the avenue below. Somehow, by means of a process I still don't understand, I'd persuaded myself that Arsène himself was responsible for what had happened that night, that, while Simin had behaved selfishly, even cruelly, he alone was to blame.

And just as I'd distanced myself from him, I'd distanced myself from her, though for a time she'd called my cell phone every night. Weeks passed, then months, when one day, just when it seemed she'd given up on me, my cell phone had buzzed.

I remember it was a Friday in June. I was meeting a woman at a restaurant in SoHo, a woman I'd only just met, and had gotten there early, briefly diverted by the sight of the waiters bustling about the well-laid tables inside, when, not thinking, I answered the call.

It was Simin. She was in France, she told me. It was late there; clearly she'd been drinking. She said she missed me very much, that she was sorry for the way she'd treated me, and pressed me to join her there, where she'd rented a house for the summer to finish some work. It would be like old times, she promised me. I could stay as long as I liked. Of course, I refused her invitation. Flustered, impatient, I told her I was busy, what with my work and with my father's failing health, a reply over which I was still puzzling, some six days later, when I boarded a flight to France.

BY NOON IT WAS hot in the park, the trees still, the air about us damp and hazy. Eager for refreshment and ready to stretch our legs, we made our way back under the busy autopista, then into the park again, on the other side, following a path past the Fountain of Netzahualcoyotl toward Chapultepec Castle, the former home of the emperor and empress, Maximilian and Carlota.

Arsène, on another occasion, one evening in Cuernavaca, where we'd sat talking on the wide, empty lawn of our hotel, had told me the story, so rich in detail, of Maximilian's arrival in Mexico City in 1863, what had marked the start of yet another empty French dream. We'd spent the afternoon that day making our way through the cluttered, brightly painted rooms of Museo Robert Brady, speaking of Francisco Toledo and Josephine Baker, and of the essays of Octavio Paz, so that for a time, after we'd returned to the hotel, our minds were not our own. It was only after we'd ordered a second drink, when the light in the trees had faded and the restaurant behind us had come alive with the sounds of talking and laughter, that he'd told me of the tragic, ill-fated reign of Fernando Maximiliano José María de Habsburgo-Lorena.

Angered by the increasingly brazen actions of Mexican President Benito Juárez, and by his refusal to settle his debts to France, Napoleon III, in league with certain members of the Mexican elite, had hatched a plan to drive Juárez out of Mexico City and replace him with a leader of their own, the artless young Maximilian, a plan they'd accomplished, roughly two years later, at the cost of some 50,000 lives.

His reign lasted just four years, when Maximilian, trapped in the city of Querétaro, to where he'd fled for his safety, was captured by Juárez and his troops, sentenced to death in a court-martial, then executed by firing squad on a site known as el Cerro de las

Campanas or 'Hill of the Bells', an event made famous by the Republican sympathizer, Édouard Manet, in his painting, *The Execution of Maximilian*, the original of which now hangs in the Kunsthalle Mannheim.

As we walked I thought about the story, about the sadness of it all, the futility, the bloodshed, the grief. And I thought about how much and how little it mattered, such history, how—how quickly now—the present supplanted the past, scattering its traces, obscuring its cufflinks and bones.

Yet it was not of Maximilian but of the architect and engineer, Felix Candela, that my friend was still thinking as we made our way through the crowded park that afternoon. He was thinking again of the time he'd spent on the grounds of Capilla Lomas de Cuernavaca, on the wide flat plain outside the city there, an experience that had troubled him deeply, he told me, as if merely resuming our conversation from that morning, when we'd stood talking on the footbridge near Casa Barragán. His time there had been so strange, so disturbing, that even that night, after he'd returned to his hotel, the well-known Las Mañanitas, where he'd made a habit of staying when in the city, he'd been too restless, too nervous to sleep.

It had been his plan to take the bus back to Mexico City the following day, where he was to meet a friend for lunch, but he'd been unable to shake his experience of the chapel, so that after breakfast the next morning, once he'd packed his bag and settled his bill, he'd hired a taxi to take him back there, though it was raining lightly and the fare, given the season, was high.

Except for some Japanese tourists, who'd soon gone their way, he'd found the grounds empty, but for a haggard old mutt with bloodshot eyes and sagging teats. Petals of pink and white flowers lay strewn about the entrance, as though some couple had just been wed.

Once inside the chapel, he'd hardly moved where he sat there beyond the potted trees, closing his eyes and listening to the rain. He'd listened to the rain, the leaves; now and then he'd heard a passing car, when suddenly he'd felt it again, the sensation, a great shuddering of feathers, of wings.

Amazed, aghast, he'd sat there for a time, for how long he couldn't say, eyes closed, counting his breaths, until at length he'd lost his bearings, his name. He remembered looking at the backs of his hands, at the veins in them, and at his shoes, which he hadn't recognized, the scuffed toes, the frayed laces. He remembered looking out beyond the altar, past Jesus on his cross, at the clouded mountains that towered above the wide, flat valley. And he remembered weeping in terror and pain.

He told me this, when for a spell we walked without talking. He clearly knew the route well (he might have walked it blindly), leading me past the frog fountain and the zoo to the bottom of Chapultepec Lake, with its food carts and vendors, where a large, overdressed family stood posing for photographs by a thick, gnarly tree.

It was crowded and noisy there, and I wondered if he would speak again, if there was more to the story of his return to the chapel, when suddenly he stammered, "It was terrifying, the feeling…" His head bobbed, his lips trembled, when loudly, miserably he groaned. I noticed his skin was flushed, he was breathing heavily, and for a moment I thought he might collapse on the ground at my feet. Instead he clutched my arm to steady himself.

He didn't look well and I was on the verge of pressing him to sit for a spell, I'd led him to a bench where a couple was sitting in the shade, but he didn't want to sit, he pushed my hand away, only to whisper, "It was frightening, and so lonely there—the rain, the chapel, the valley. With the wind blowing, with the rain beating down, I could hardly think or breathe. I rocked, I whimpered, I hadn't the strength to cry out. I understood it was me and not me, for you see I was certain I'd been there before, that then was now, that I was sitting, not in the chapel as it is today, surrounded by houses, apartments, and shops, but in the chapel as it *was,* as I'd seen it depicted in the grainy reproductions in this book on Candela I'd found, photographs taken (perhaps by Candela himself) shortly after the chapel's completion in 1958.

"I remember feeling dizzy, sick. And I remember thinking about my mother; I remember gazing up into the stark, quadric shell of the chapel and knowing in my heart she was dead." He was silent for a moment, seemingly distracted by the family beside us, only to remark, "They were shot to death in the woods outside of Vienna."

"Who was?" I asked, confused.

"Her parents, my mother's parents. They were dragged from their apartment one night and forced to kneel in the mud where they were made to pray, though they'd never prayed, though they'd never given a thought to God. My mother was in Paris at the time, holding hands with my father by the Seine."

I didn't see the connection, but was accustomed to his eccentric way of speaking, and was on the verge of asking him to elaborate, to explain, for I'd never heard the story, when softly he said, "Sitting there in the chapel that morning, it was as if I could remember the very quality of the light, the air, the day those photographs were taken, though it would be another four years until I was even born—two weeks late and with an atrial septal defect in a dark Franciscan hospital in Neuilly-sur-Seine!"

He told me he'd often suffered such impressions, the feeling in a place that he was there and not there, or rather that he was there but had been there before, as a different person with a different pair of eyes. Of course, the experience was not unique; over the years he'd met dozens of people who'd made similar claims, some of which had seemed extraordinary when compared to his own.

"Mind you, there was nothing religious about the experience," he hastened to add.   "The chapel might have been a theatre or a bus stop; it might have been a factory for the production of rum. What moved me that day was the architecture alone, the sense, there beneath the high cross curves of the shell, that time itself had been freed."

The remark made him chuckle; he wasn't sure what he meant by it, only that it had felt something like that.

From there we followed a wide, shaded path in the direction of Cuauhtémoc and Anzures before looping northward toward Colonia Polanco, the fancy, glass-fronted buildings of which we could see through the trees. Punctuated by dark outcroppings of rock, the area through which we strolled was the oldest part of the park, Arsène explained to me, pointing this way and that. "It was here that the Aztecs first settled after their wanderings through the land, a site that later, when Tenochtitlán was thriving, became popular among their rulers as a summer retreat, the portraits of some of whom can still be seen on the eastern slope of Chapultepec Hill."

He walked more slowly than he had at the start, he

paused more often, his feet seemed to drag. At points he appeared lost in his thoughts.

I was still thinking about Candela's chapel, and at a break in the conversation I asked him about the man himself, about his early life in Spain, intrigued by this devotee of Ortega y Gasset, this 'Moor', and eager to know more about the forces that had brought him here, to Mexico, where he'd married, raised a family, and made himself a name.

A Republican during the Civil War, Candela had been assigned to the Works Command Post in Albacete, explained Arsène, clearly pleased be able to flesh out the man for me. "His job was to restore and remodel buildings for military use, though almost at once he was transferred to Gerona as captain of a battalion of works and fortifications, where, among other things, he was charged with building access roads to Ebro through the rugged limestone hills.

"Yet his efforts were largely in vain, for soon thereafter the Republicans were forced to retreat across the French border, where Candela, along with his fellow soldiers, was captured by the French Army and confined to a concentration camp near Perpignan. There he waited in boredom and despair. Then one day, after weeks of hearing rumors that he and his compatriots would be returned to Spain, to Franco and his henchmen, he was informed he'd been chosen by lottery to emigrate to Mexico instead, though he'd never put his name on the list.

"Of course, Mexico had seemed like a dream to him. After twenty-one days at sea, he'd arrived in the steamy port of Veracruz on June 13th, 1939, aboard the French cargo ship, *Sinaia*, and had been struck at once by the happy, generous feeling in the air, by the sense that the nation was just rousing itself after a long and fitful sleep. Indeed, he'd found the people here eager for change, impatient to make a break with the past, a desire that recently had fueled a veritable explosion in construction throughout the country.

"It seemed his luck had finally changed. You see, not only had there been a dramatic increase in building by the time of his arrival, but the labor was cheap, and the use of concrete—his material of choice—was considered both efficient and modern. What's more, the Mexican building codes were less restrictive than those in Spain, giving him greater freedom to experiment with his designs. What more could a brilliant young architect have asked for than that?

"Yet the experience was hardly his alone, not by far," said Arsène, as we made our way beneath the overhanging trees. "An estimated 25,000 Spaniards fled here to Mexico during and immediately following the Spanish Civil War, the majority of them settling in and around the capital here, where, despite the reservations of many Mexicans, for many had protested their arrival, the erstwhile refugees soon contributed widely to the life and spirit of the city."

He himself had only learned about them recently, Arsène told me, while he was working as a consultant at the Instituto Nacional de Psiquiatría Dr. Ramón de la Fuente Muñiz. It was during that time that he'd met a young woman named Flavia Morales, a patient suffering from depression, whose lita, or grandmother, an art historian and madrileña named Maria Altolaguirre, had fled the violence of Franco, first to France, to Paris, then here—via Veracruz—to Mexico City.

It was in her late grandmother's apartment, one floor of a crumbling French-style mansion in Colonia San Rafael, that the young woman, Flavia, had lived.

"Had?" I asked him.

"Yes, she killed herself one day. She'd tried it before, to gas herself in the kitchen there. There was little we could do." He paused for a moment, when he shook his head. "She was very proud of her grandmother, of the books she'd written, of the art she'd collected, at least some of which she'd smuggled out of Spain. It was remarkable, really: everywhere you turned there were paintings, photographs, and books."

"So, you saw it yourself, the apartment?"

"Oh yes, many times," he replied. "As I was not her doctor, at least not officially, we felt perfectly at ease with each other. She could really make me laugh." The recollection brought a smile to his lips, when, taking me by the arm, he said, "That was the first I'd heard of these refugees from Spain, of whom, of course, our Candela was one."

"Then the two of them must have known each other!" I suggested, for suddenly it seemed obvious to me.

Oddly it had never occurred to him, so that he stopped in his tracks. "Why, I haven't the faintest idea!" he cried. "Flavia never mentioned it to me, though you're right, they must have known each other. After all it was not a large community here, and by the early 1950's Candela's name was on everyone's lips," he added, only to remark with a grin, "Then again, so was hers! For if Candela was famous in his adopted homeland, Maria Altolaguirre was possibly even more so, or at least equally, differently so!"

"Do you mean, in the world of art history?"

"Yes, in the world of art history, surely, but in other

ways, too. In a matter of years, she'd not only turned her back on Spain, on Franco and his fascists, as well as on Murillo, Velázquez, and Goya, but had focused her writing, her attention, on the riches right here in Mexico, on the people, the culture, the food, the art, all of which she'd traveled the length of the country to see. She was zealous in her interests, her charms, drinking and smoking, hobnobbing with artists, writers, and politicians, and indulging herself in any number of highly publicized affairs, with men, yes, but mostly with women, the framed, sometimes naked photographs of whom she'd adorned her bedroom walls.

"Not surprisingly, she'd been a controversial figure in this staunchly Catholic land, heckled and harassed, suspended from her post at the university, and even threatened with arrest. And the newspapers had loved her," he remarked with delight, "filling their pages with her antics, her face!"

Flavia had showed him the clippings, which her grandmother had collected over the years in a large cardboard box, the cartoons and photographs meant to shame her, as well as the many articles, letters, and editorials in which she—a professor, art historian, and philanthropist, a woman who'd devoted the better part of her life to extolling the virtues, the *genius*, of

Mexico—had been oppugned and reviled almost weekly as a lesbian and homewrecker, as a communist, an atheist, a Jew.

"Marimacha was the term they'd used most often to describe her," he told me. "I must have seen it a dozen times in the brown and brittle clippings, though in her appearance, her demeanor, she was anything but manly. Rather, she appeared to have adopted a kind of mocking, *hyper*-femininity, more woman than woman, it seemed! She'd worn dresses, always, kept her hair long, made a fetish of bracelets and rings. She'd loved perfume and lipstick, high heels. And she was beautiful—conventionally, even classically so, if such terms mean anything these days."

He was quiet for a spell, when he said, "It saddens me to think of her now, to realize that, with the death of her granddaughter, there isn't anyone to know her anymore, to remember her struggle, her life." I saw him shake his head then smile. "Though perhaps she's not to be pitied. According to Flavia she'd hardly suffered at all, but had laughed and sung about it every step of the way!

"Still she must have had her sorrows, her doubts. She died in her bed one night at the age of ninety-three."

"Did she ever regret leaving Spain?" I asked him, when he paused for a moment to catch his breath.

"Perhaps, but I don't think so," he replied. "No doubt she missed certain people, certain things. We all do. Yet according to Flavia, she'd never been tempted to return, not actually, not even after Franco died. She'd said his death was not enough.

"Still, that hadn't prevented her from imagining such a trip; in fact, she and Flavia had made a game of it in the years before her death, drawing up lists of the many places they'd visit while there, of the foods they'd eat, of the people—celebrities mostly—whose doorbells they'd ring. They'd planned to start in Madrid, first always Madrid, where her grandmother would show her the building in which she'd lived as a girl, the university at which she'd studied, and the cafés where she'd spent the evenings and weekends with her friends.

"There at the large table in her kitchen, she and Flavia had studied the city with the aid of maps she'd ordered through a local bookstore, wandering the streets together, many of the names of which had been changed since Franco's death, so that they'd often gotten lost. Gone were Calle Primero de Octubre, Calle del Puerto de leones, and Pasaje del General Mola; gone were Calle del General Verela, Calle del Comandante Zorita, and Calle del Almirante Francisco Moreno; gone too were Avenida del Arco de la Victoria, Plaza del Veintiocho de Marzo, and Plaza del Caudillo. Yet what had pleased her grandmother most (for she read the Spanish papers) was the talk of exhuming Franco's remains. She'd hoped they'd be dumped in the street somewhere, any old street, then washed down the drain with a hose!"

Flavia had told him that and more, as she'd led him through the large, cluttered rooms of the apartment, opening cupboards and cabinets and drawers. She'd worried greatly about what to do with her grandmother's things, the paintings and sculptures, the pottery and baskets, the books and photographs, the brooches and bracelets and rings. It had kept her up at night to think about it, had made her tremble and weep, so that often she'd paced the marble floors until daylight, when the traffic rose up and she heard the birds in the trees.

"In the months before she killed herself she'd begun to catalogue the various pieces, though in truth she'd hardly begun, given the sheer volume of *things*. I'd recommended she hire a professional to do it, I'd even offered to pay the fee, until she was back on her feet, but she'd been adamant about doing it herself. She didn't trust people and never took money from anyone. In any case, she'd told me, she had nothing else to do.

"You see, by then, by the time I got to know her, she'd quit her job in a local supermarket," he explained, "though she may very well have been fired. The way she talked, it was hard to tell, she was often so angry, so sad. She'd trained as a nurse, had worked for a spell in a pediatric unit, then had gotten into an argument with her boss, a man she'd been dating for years. She'd discovered one day that he had a wife and children, and that he'd never had any intention of marrying her. She'd often dreamt of killing him, she'd told me, of using a nail file to gouge out his eyes, but it was only talk, she'd assured me. She'd hadn't the courage for that."

"So, what ever happened to her grandmother's things?"

"I have no idea," he replied, ruefully. "I'd already returned to New York when I learned of Flavia's death. Anxious to know, I'd sent a friend to investigate, but by the time he'd managed to speak with the landlord the apartment was empty."

By THEN HIS FACE and neck were blotchy from the heat, his eyes a bit glassy, so that, after seeing him settled on a bench outside the entrance to the botanical garden, I bought him a bottle of water to drink. He'd been so eager to see me that morning he'd neglected to eat breakfast. It was foolish, he knew.

He suggested we rest there for a while, then wander over to the anthropological museum, where the rooms were dark and cool. Some years before we'd spent the better part of a day there together, admiring the exhibits and talking by the great fountain in the courtyard. He wanted to show me one of his favorite pieces there, the head of a macaw carved in stone, a piece so brilliant, so suggestive, he claimed, one could practically hear it laughing!

IT WAS WHILE WE were sitting there, distracted by the people milling by, that Arsène mentioned to me the fact that he'd recently encountered our friend David, whom he hadn't seen in months.

"David?" I gasped, barely able to conceal my astonishment. Was it true? No, he must be toying with me… Was it possible he didn't know? I searched his face for a sign, a flicker in the eye, a curl of the lip, anything that might give him away, but he wasn't even looking at me. Instead he was polishing his glasses.

I was staggered. It defied belief; it beggared all reason, all sense. I was certain Simin had told him everything—about her and David, about *me*. She'd never been one to hold back.

Aghast, I looked at him again. He'd just finished the bottle of water I'd gotten for him and closed his eyes with an appreciative sigh. Clearly, Simin had told him of her affair. Had she simply withheld her lover's name? Had she spared him that one, that abominable detail? And if so, *why*? It wasn't like her at all.

And what about me? I wondered. She must have told him something about me.

"Yes, it was quite a surprise," said Arsène. "There I was waiting for the shuttle one evening, the station was very crowded, when suddenly David tapped me on the shoulder! Good old David! Handsome as ever, though he looked older to me, somehow, perhaps a little tired. He joked and smiled as usual, asking about Simin and Élise—and about *you*," he added, as if just remembering it. "He thought you'd dropped off the face of the earth."

"He asked about *me*?" The thought was disconcerting.

"Yes, he was eager to know what you'd been up to. He wondered if you were still in New York. Of course, I told him what I knew, what little that was, for by then we'd all but lost touch with you. And that's when he said a funny thing…"

"What funny thing?" I must have looked alarmed because he patted my arm.

"Oh nothing, nothing bad. It was just a bit odd, what he said, even for David. I'm still not sure what he meant."

"Well, what did he say? Was he talking about me?"

"Yes, we were talking about you, your work, your travels, when suddenly, raising a finger like an actor, he cocked his head and cried, 'The cheat has flown the roost!' Do you know the line? It's from *Tosca*, I looked it up, though for the life of me I can't see the connection, the point. But no matter," he said with a shrug. "That's David for you, strange man. He said he'd be sure to track you down."

"Track me down? What does he want with me?"

"I suppose just to catch up. He said it had been months since he'd seen you, that you hadn't answered his calls."

"Yes, that's true. He called me once or twice, back in April, I think, but I've been busy travelling and taking care of my father." Despite my effort to remain calm, I found David's interest in me disturbing.

"How *is* your father?" said Arsène.

"Fine. At least as well as can be expected. So, what else did he tell you?" I pressed him, sternly. "When you met him in the station. What else did David say?"

"David? Well, not much, really. As I mentioned, it was only for a matter of minutes that we spoke. He was in a hurry, you see...and the noise! You know the noise down there. In the end he didn't even get on the train, but took the stairs to the street again."

"You mean, he changed his mind?"

"Apparently so," said Arsène. "You know he works near there. Perhaps he'd just forgotten something. A file, his phone. Perhaps he'd just decided to walk home."

"To 103rd Street? I thought you said it was raining."

"No, it wasn't raining, I'm sure of it. It was a bright, sunny day. I'd eaten my lunch in the park."

"So, he didn't say anything else? Nothing at all?"

"No, nothing I can remember."

DAVID TROUBLED ME. HE always had. Though we'd been friends for years, at least friends of a sort, I'd long felt he didn't trust me, my opinion of him, my presence, that he was watching me out of the corner of his eye. What was clear, what had always been clear, was that he was puzzled, even threatened, by my relationship with Simin. For a time, before he'd had sex with her, he'd tried to make me his confidante, his ally, pulling me aside at a concert or party to grill me about her, her friends, her interests, her habits, even pressing me to tell him about her body itself, which he'd assumed I'd seen and knew, lewd, often prurient questions about her buttocks and breasts. He would ask me such things, eyes ablaze, face flushed, he would pace and moan and bite his fist, only to curse her as a harpy, a cock-tease, a bitch.

For the two of them had argued incessantly, whenever they'd met, smiling and chuckling at each other, as they circled the room with their drinks. They'd disagreed about everything—about women and politics, about restaurants and movies, about the future of healthcare in France, so that often, by the time Simin had shut the door behind him of an evening, she'd been sick with loathing and rage.

He was convinced that I was privy to her inner life, her secrets, her dreams, and had beseeched me endlessly to tell him what I knew of her—of her marriage and sex life, of what she said about *him*. Some nights, after we'd all been together in Simin and Arsène's apartment, eating and drinking, he'd waited in the lobby for me, or beneath the wide green awning out front, anxious, eager to hear my accounting of the night, joking with me, clapping me on the back of the neck, even calling a taxi for us, if it was raining or cold, so that we could talk at our leisure, in peace. He was relentless in his efforts to crack the code of her, which he was convinced I could help him to do.

He didn't love her, she must have known it; he'd wanted only to fuck her, to subject and subdue her, to beat her at her game. That was how he was. For all his salacious talk, for all the obscenities he'd whispered in my ear, what he'd wanted, finally, what he'd wanted more than sex, was to tame her, her spirit, to master her composure, her will.

For months I'd watched him at work on her, as one watches a fisherman on tv, the sort who fishes for sport, had seen the way, upon sinking the hook in her lip, he'd let her run with the line for a while, teasing her, acknowledging a parry, even conceding a point, if the occasion seemed right, only to reel her in, slowly but surely, just a bit at a time, so that she'd hardly felt a thing. He was sedulous in this, coldly, almost preternaturally so, repeating the process night after night, drink after drink, party after party, until, there on the rooftop, he was licking the salt from her skin.

I'd tried to warn her, many times; of him and his intentions I'd spoken bluntly, in no uncertain terms. She'd simply chosen to ignore me, to laugh it off, to pretend I'd imagined it all, contending, in any case, that I needn't worry about her. She could take care of herself.

After all, she knew his kind well, she'd insisted to me one evening, when we'd stood drinking in her kitchen. She'd assured me that he could never manipulate her, not David, he wasn't smart enough for that. It didn't matter that he'd actually told me what he was doing, and *how*, that more than once he'd boasted to me about his progress with her, at one point actually offering to bet me that soon, very soon, he'd have her naked on her knees. She'd found it amusing, my concern. Tucking her hair behind her ears, she'd smiled strangely at me. It didn't matter that I'd seen him do it before, with other women, and often in much less time, that he'd been doing it successfully, without compunction, for years. It didn't matter *what* I told her—and I told her everything, that he was callous and cunning, that he didn't give a damn about her, her thoughts, her feelings, that he was ruthless and selfish and cruel. My words, my warnings, she was deaf to them, teasing me, indulging me, before dismissing it all with a pat on my cheek. And still I'd struggled to persuade her: I'd ranted and raved, I'd practically frothed at the mouth in my effort to make her hear me, to *see*.

"Now you're being silly," she'd told me at one point, leading me back into the living room, where she'd settled herself on the couch with her wine and cigarettes. "Remember, I've known David for years, almost as long as you have. I know all of his foibles, his tricks. So, he wants to fuck me, big deal. Lots of men do. So, he thinks he can hustle me, that he can sway me with his arrogance, his muscles, his dick. Fine, then let him think so. Let him think he's the king of the world, for all I care, but understand this: no one is going to *make* me do anything. Sure, Arsène and I have had our problems, but that doesn't mean I'm going to jump into bed with the first man who winks at me."

"But, Simin, I wasn't suggesting that at all," I'd replied. "You can do what you like, with whomever you choose. I don't care. I'm only talking about *David*, no one else, about one particular man."

It was then that she'd cocked her head at me. "You really don't like him, do you?"

"Don't like him? We've been friends forever. This has nothing to do with me," I'd protested, gulping the last of my wine.

"Listen, I've seen the way he treats you."

"What do you mean?"

"The way he mocks and belittles you, the way he bullies you about your sex life, your 'girlfriends', the way he put you in a headlock the other night and made you fight to get free."

"Sure, he's a prick, a real bastard sometimes. But everyone knows that."

"Yes, but he picks on you the most. Every time we're together, it seems. If I were you I'd hate his fucking guts."

"Well you're *not* me, and I *don't!*" I'd snapped at her, rising abruptly from the couch. "Think what you like, Simin. Whatever the hell you like. I'm simply trying to warn you."

AFTER THAT, WHENEVER SHE'D pressed me to tell her about David, I'd refused to speak to her, to be drawn out by her questions, her appeals. That night in her kitchen, I'd learned my lesson, once again. I'd made the mistake that night of speaking frankly to her, of committing myself to a position with her, a habit I'd broken some years before, for the pain and anguish it had caused me. It was a mistake I'd vowed never to repeat, no matter what she told me, no matter how she pleaded, no matter how she suffered or bled. I would not be tempted, I would not be drawn in.

Yet even the best-laid plans go awry. The night she'd called me after having had sex with David on their roof, I'd found myself helpless to refuse her, to resist the strange, dark charm of her voice. For all the bitterness she stirred in me, I was more in love with her than ever.

I remember I was sitting at my desk. It was warm out, the window was open, I could hear the traffic on the avenue below. I was working on the introduction to my translation of Sergio Pitol's *The Art of Flight*, and had gotten distracted by the section in his memoir-novel in which he writes about his own translation of the novel *Behind the Door* by the Jewish-Italian author, Giorgio Bassini, a story, a project, that had interested him very little, he'd claimed, though he'd needed the money. He was living in Barcelona at the time and hating it—the schedule, the waiting, the noise. His stomach hurt, he was broke, and he'd been sleeping poorly. I was thinking about Pitol in Barcelona, and about Bassini, the nostalgic Bassini, when my cell phone buzzed.

It had been weeks since I'd spoken with Simin, so that it had come as a shock to think of her again, to picture her face, to recall in an instant the thrill and affliction of her voice. Of late, I'd hardly thought of her at all, but as a feature of some other, distant life. I'd not only been reading and writing with a greater clarity than I had in years, but I'd been seeing a woman, a German, with whom, just recently, I'd spent a restful vacation in Spain. The last thing I needed was Simin.

"Hello?" I said.

"Listen, I'm sorry. I know it's late, but I just have to tell someone."

"So, WHAT DO YOU think?" said Arsène, startling me from my thoughts, where we sat resting on the bench. He was studying me with a quizzical look, as if he'd been talking for some time.

"Think?" I replied. "About what?"

"About David, his divorce."

"His divorce? When? What happened?"

"I'm sorry. I'd assumed you'd heard. It was some months ago. Apparently, his wife found out he'd been cheating on her."

"Does Simin know?" I asked, before I could catch myself.

"Simin? I suppose so. He's thinking of moving to Berlin. For years his firm has been pressuring him to relocate there."

"So, is that what he's planning to do?"

"I couldn't say, though it would probably be good for him—you know, a change of scenery, of air. No doubt that's why he'd like to see you again, to tell you about his plans."

"It's a shame, really," was all I managed to reply, for my mind was racing. Surely David didn't think I was the one who'd told his wife, that she'd learned about it from me. Why, I hardly knew her, Sophia, she'd never joined our parties, he'd never invited her.

She was always busy, tied up, always happy at home with their kids. In any case, what did I care? He could do what he liked. I wasn't his keeper, his conscience. And why now? Why would I have told his wife *now*, when he'd been sleeping with Simin for years? It made no sense. Had I wished to expose him, to humiliate him, I would have done so long ago, when my umbrage and outrage were clear. Surely he knows that, that it was someone else who'd told her, perhaps someone who'd seen them in the street one day and had recognized the signs—the smiles, the deference, the hand on the back, some neighbor or friend who'd finally screwed up the courage to speak to her, to pull her aside, to tell her what she'd seen, for one's friends and neighbors are often the first to detect such things, though they rarely share them with us, how could they, they would hurt us, we might turn on them in our anger and pain.

Or perhaps no one had told her. Perhaps she herself had discovered them by accident, by chance, it was possible, for eventually everyone slips up, gets cocky, no matter how prudent, how careful they've been, some lipstick on his collar, some text or photo on his phone. Who knows, she might have seen them together in the street one day or in the park in the sunshine or in the window of some restaurant or bar. She might have spied them getting out of a taxi one evening, the two of them laughing, the two of them drunk, she might have seen them entering the lobby of some midtown hotel and followed them inside, even that is more likely.

That I myself am to blame—why, no one would believe it, least of all David. It's not in my nature, not me. He couldn't possibly think that I was the one who'd betrayed him, that I'd patiently bided my time all these years, watching and waiting, that I'd chosen now, of all occasions, to expose him, to confront his wife, his poor, unwitting wife, approaching her in the street one day or in the lobby of their building, where I'd found her searching her purse for her keys. He couldn't possibly believe that I would hazard such a thing, that I'd had the wits, the *righteousness*, to confront her, this woman I barely know, this lawyer, this mother of two, with her lipstick and pearls, whom I've only ever met but once, in passing, at a restaurant downtown.

Then again, perhaps he doesn't think I confronted her at all, at least not in person, but sent her a letter instead, an anonymous letter, or, better yet, that I called her on her cell phone one night when I knew that he was out, that she was alone in their apartment, reading, working, or finishing up the dishes, some evening after she'd put the children to bed and had dimmed the lights, when perhaps she'd removed her shoes and had poured herself a glass of whiskey and was standing at the window looking out at the dark, sluggish river and at the rain-lashed park below, thinking vaguely of some case that was troubling her, some client, of the talking on the radio in the kitchen, of the stubborn winter dryness of her skin. Hello. Who's calling? she'd say, her voice a little hoarse, uneasy, for the hour would be late, the park empty, the rain thrumming hard against the windows where she stood. Certain names would spring to mind, certain faces. She'd stammer, catch her breath, for always one is helpless when one answers the phone: it could be anything or nothing, she'd know.

In a flash, in that gaping interregnum before I spoke, she'd imagine such things, good things and bad things, but mostly bad things, mostly tragic, one cannot help it, one thinks the worst, the things least likely, for the odds mean nothing at night. Was it David? Had something happened to David? Had her sister crashed her car? The seconds would stretch to minutes, hours, her vision would narrow, the room around her lose its nature, its shape. There'd be nothing she could do but stand there and wait, her cell phone pressed to one ear. Not even if the earth shook beneath her could she move an inch from where she stood, could she set down her drink, could she check on the children in their beds. Having answered the call and not recognized the number, the name, she'd be forced to stand there forever—at least until I spoke, until I told her who I was and why I'd called, when I'd be helpless to stop myself, though she wept and trembled, though she cursed me, though she threatened to hang up the phone.

Once I started there'd be no way for her to resist what I was telling her, what my mouth was saying, no way to stem the dark, septic flow of my words, which would rush like a toxin through her veins, constricting her muscles and lungs. Once I'd begun, there'd be nothing she could do to save herself from hearing me, to redress the present, the past, no means to stop up her ears, to avert the dreadful onslaught of my words, a call she'd known was coming, she'd known and rehearsed it for years, a tale, a story, someone was bound to tell her one day, some night when David was gone and the kids were asleep, when it was dark out and raining, when at last she'd allowed her worries to wander, to trickle off and fade, she'd sensed it would be then, when she'd let down her guard, after she'd poured herself a whiskey and taken off her shoes, it would be then that her cell phone would ring, at such a moment, on such a night, when she was feeling tired and lonely, when she was thinking about her work or about the laundry to fold or about the children's lunches to be made, it would happen then, only then, when she'd convinced herself it didn't matter anymore, what he'd done, let come what will, what may, when the hurt and anger had subsided, when she'd grown bored of her doubts and suspicions, when at last she felt too worldly, too weary to care.

She'd sensed it would be then, at such a moment, on such a night, that her cell phone would ring, that someone like me would call her, some stranger with an ax to grind (against David, against her), someone who reveled in cruelty and gossip, or else (she'd have considered this, too) it would be someone she knew and loved, a friend or colleague or neighbor, perhaps just an acquaintance, some person she'd met but once, at a crowded new restaurant downtown, someone who pitied her, her position, some man or woman who knew things, *too much*, and had suffered them too long. She'd sensed it would be some such person who would call her one night, if not a rival or gossip, then someone lonely and anxious like her, someone weary of what he knew, of what he must tell her, for her sake, for *his*, someone who wanted only what was best for her, she was young, still able, she with her children, her friends, she had beauty and courage and means...

ARSÈNE HAD GOTTEN TO his feet; clearly, he was feeling better, for he suggested we continue our walk, that we make our way to the anthropological museum. Occasionally his hands trembled, as he spoke; I'd noticed it before, when we'd stood talking about Candela on the footbridge near Casa Barragán, a dancing of the fingers that had made me think he was tapping out a beat.

Hat in hand, he was telling me about the long and colorful history of the Mexico City flâneur, a tradition at least as old as that of Paris. Literary, eclectic, the practice had begun in the early sixteenth century, he explained to me, when the chroniclers of the Spanish conquest of Mexico, mostly soldiers and priests, had written lavishly of their strolls through the dazzling Aztec capital.

"Through their accounts of Tenochtitlán one sees again the sparkling blue lake waters with their floating gardens," he whispered, sweeping his hand before him as if to recreate the scene for me, "the grid-like network of chinampas or canals, and the great white city of Motecuhzoma itself, every building—the houses, villas, and palaces—plastered thickly with lime. They, the Spanish, found a city of mighty temples, open-air markets, and finely cobbled streets lined with colorful shrubs, fragrant roses, and sweet-smelling trees. To the conquistador and early chronicler, Bernal Diaz del Castillo, what he beheld here seemed as marvelous, as enchanted, as a scene from the tale of Amadis.

"Of course, you know the rest," he added, after a pause. "Once destroyed by the Spanish, the great Aztec city was rebuilt and reimagined according to their spiteful, often garish tastes. Not content to merely augment what they found, they murdered the people, destroyed the temples, and filled in the canals. Upon the ruins of Tenochtitlán they built their palaces, convents, and churches; with God and violence they raised a phoenix from the ashes here, a fact, a vision, immortalized by the priest and poet Bernardo de Balbuena in his 1604 epic, *La grandeza mexicana*—O 'center of perfection'! O 'hinge of the world'!

"Written in the epistolary style, in reply to a letter from a nun named Isabel de Tovar y Guzman, who'd asked the priest for a description of the burgeoning new city, the poem is in essence a lyrical, at points apophatic inventory of what he'd found in this 'nueva Roma', in this 'teatro de fortuna', avid, often baroque descriptions of its multifarious wonders: its buildings, peoples, trades, goods, art forms, animals, political and religious practices, and, of course, its natural bounty: the riot of fruits and vegetables, the pageant of flowers and trees. The place he described for her is remarkable—at once a utopian dreamspace, an idealized garden of flowering, fragrant beauty, and a bustling metropolis, a clearinghouse of goods and services, a gritty hub of commerce and exchange!"

Not surprisingly, Arsène knew the opening stanza by heart:

> Si al graue curso del feliz gouierno,
> En que de vn nueuo mundo la gran masa
> Con tu saber y tu grandeza mides,
> El passo cortas y el ferbor diuides,
> Y vn pecho tan prudente como tierno,
> Da aliuio al tiempo, a los cuydados tassa,
> Nueuo Meçenas, gloria de la casa
> Mas noble, y mas antigua
> Que España en sus Archiuos atestigua,
> Pues siglos vence, y las edades passa,
> Passe tambien, y crezca como espuma,
> Mi humilde yedra, que en su exselso muro,
> Busca arrimo seguro,
> Donde ni la marchite, ni consuma,
> El inuidioso aliento que procura
> Manchar el Sol, y hazer su lumbre escura.

AND SO HE TALKED as we made our way along the path to the crowded museum entrance, outside of which we settled ourselves on a bench to rest.

To pass the time, while we waited for a large class of schoolchildren to enter the museum, he told me about the first modern chroniclers of Mexico City, about the turn-of-the-last-century dandy, Artemio de Valle Arizpe, and about Salvador Novo, a brash young poet who'd fancied himself a cross between Oscar Wilde and André Gide. It was Novo who'd taken on the challenge of rewriting Balbuena's epic poem about the city, adding art deco neighborhoods, art nouveau apartment buildings, and a fleet of roaring Packards, Cadillacs, and Chevrolets. Then there were the novels *La región más transparente* by Carlos Fuentes, *Y retiemble en sus centros la tierra* by Gonzalo Celerio, and *Los detectives salvajes* by Roberto Bolaño, as well as the urban, anti-rhetorical poetry of Efraín Huerta.

"And that was only the beginning," he exclaimed, for there were many more such splendid accountings of the city to come, works like *City of Palaces* by Guillermo Tovar de Teresa, *Down and Delirious in Mexico City* by Daniel Hernandez, *First Stop in the New World* by David Lida, *Mexico City Noir* by Paco Ignacio Taibo II, *Secret Mexico City* by Yair Lobo, *Las reinas de Polanco* by Guadalupe Loaeza, *City on a Lake* by Matthew Vitz, *The Interior Circuit: A Mexico City Chronicle* by Francisco Goldman, *Among Strange Victims* by Daniel

Saldaña París, *Return to Centro Histórico* by Ilan Stavans, and, most recently, the novel *La Historia de mis dientes* by Valeria Luiselli, the story of a man, an auctioneer, named Gustavo "Highway" Sánchez Sánchez who wanders through the industrial suburbs of the city smiling at everyone he meets with what he believes to be the actual teeth of Marilyn Monroe! Arsène had read them all, he told me, and with each account—every one of them—he'd seen the city anew.

The schoolchildren were restless where they stood waiting in the sun, and for a few moments we watched them teasing and poking each other, when, adjusting his pack on his lap, Arsène continued his history of the Mexico City flâneur by speaking of the empress herself. "She wrote vividly about the city," he told me, "letters mostly, in which she described for her family and friends back in Europe the many wonders she beheld in her daily carriage rides through the streets here, and in her outings on horseback in the early mornings through the dark, cool forests of tamarisk, cedar, and pine.

"It was on one such morning, while out riding with Maximilian, here in Chapultepec, in what was mostly forest with a network of soft sandy paths, that they'd chanced upon an old mansion on the bluff there," he said, gesturing vaguely through the trees, "what was then but a characterless pile that had been neglected for years. Built high upon the rock face by the Spanish viceroys in the late eighteenth century, it had been used, in subsequent years, as a barracks, a hospital, and as a military college, before being abandoned altogether, sometime after the Mexican-American War. Delighted by their discovery, the emperor and his young empress (for she was only twenty-four) had spent the morning exploring the dank, empty rooms with their broken tiles and peeling walls, with their stench of pigeon dung and urine, and admiring the views from the many ruined windows, from one of which, over the tops of the trees through which they'd just ridden, they could gaze out over the vast southeastern plain to the lakes and distant fields, and to the great slumbering volcanoes, the mythical Nahua warrior, Popocatépetl, and his beloved princess, Iztaccíhuatl.

"She captured all of it in her letters," explained Arsène, dabbing at his forehead with his handkerchief, "her excitement, her amazement. It seemed a fairy tale to her, the people, the city, an adventure too good to be true."

Wiping his face with his handkerchief, he said, "She loved it all. Truly. Yet it was by Chapultepec here that she was particularly charmed, and quickly persuaded

Maximilian to move the seat of his court here, far from the hustle and bustle of the city. To the ambitious young emperor, it seemed a timely, portentous idea, eager as he was to establish himself as emperor in his new homeland, to impress himself upon his subjects, so that he wasted no time in having the place renovated. Using his own architect and interior designer (and a veritable army of Mexican workers), he soon replaced the viceroys' modest mansion with an enormous French-style castle with colonnades, verandas, arcades, and a wide covered terrace from which in the evenings they could admire the views. His vision was exacting, so that he quickly transformed the rooms inside—those that were already there, and those that were new—with shiploads of furniture, artwork, and carpeting from Europe, all in a neoclassical style. With the aid of an Austrian botanist named Wilhelm Knechtel he built a garden on the roof. Finally, to connect their new home to the capital, he ordered the construction of a long avenue, bordered with eucalyptus trees, which he named Paseo de la Emperatriz.

"Needless to say, young Charlotte was thrilled, though her pleasure proved short-lived, for the tale was in fact too good to be true.'

"How so?" I asked. "Was it Juárez?'

"Juárez, yes, though he didn't really start to trouble them until later. The problem was Maximilian himself. Just as he and the empress were beginning to establish a routine here, in their sumptuous new retreat, to develop their love for one another, he decided to undertake a lengthy tour of the provinces without her. Hurt, and not a little surprised, she accepted his charge to preside over the council of ministers in his absence, a responsibility largely symbolic, which, however, due to a host of unforeseen emergencies while he was away, had required her to assume a veritable regency in his place.

"Accordingly, she met with councilors, delivered speeches, held public audiences, presided over charitable ceremonies, and inspected institutions. So avid was her intelligence, so hungry did she feel for the work, that each night she locked herself away in her rooms to read texts on politics, history, economics, and law. She found she excelled in financial matters, particularly, working closely with Maximilian's deputies to clarify and stabilize the country's economy, which by any measure was a formidable task. Her days were long and hard. Still, she'd never felt better, worthier of her position, her title, and could hardly wait for Maximilian to return to tell him all she'd done.

"When at last he did return, when, finally, she had a

chance to speak with him alone, he did not seem pleased with her news. Indeed, the next time he left her in power, as he would do regularly in the months and years to come, he did so only after strictly curtailing her powers. All civilian and military cabinet reports would still go to Charlotte, but only he himself would be permitted to sign them. Furthermore, she was forbidden to take part in any matters dealing with legislation, nominations, promotions, diplomatic correspondence, extra-budgetary expenditures, troop maneuvers, and judicial affairs. As empress she was free to give public audiences, visit charitable foundations and schools, and open correspondence from Europe, as long as it was not addressed to Maximilian marked 'private' or 'personal'. Finally, she was no longer permitted to enter his office unannounced.

"Some—those who don't believe she was poisoned—say that that was when her madness began..." remarked Arsène with a distant, somber tone, when abruptly, seizing my arm, he pointed to the museum entrance through which the last of the schoolchildren were filing. "Quick! Now's our chance. I want to show you that macaw."

INSIDE THE MUSEUM IT was dark and cool, so that it took a few moments for our eyes to adjust to the space.

He found the macaw at once, in a gallery labeled "The Toltecs and the Epiclassic". Made of polished gray stone, the sculpture had been discovered near the ruins of Xochicalco, about a half an hour drive from Cuernavaca. "See what I mean?" he said. "It's brilliant, isn't it? Such playfulness, such humor!"

"So, what did Carlota do?" I asked him, at length, after we'd toured the gallery and had returned to the Central Patio. The sun was strong, so that we stood to the side in the shade. "How did she respond?"

"Why, she did the only thing she *could* do: she bowed her head and complied, though she was restless and miserable, pacing the palace's empty halls, pulling at her hair, and tearing at her handkerchiefs with her teeth. She felt misprized, misjudged. After all, Maximilian had *asked* her to do it; it was only to please him that she'd agreed to govern in his stead.

"Yet the damage had been done. She knew it. Without intending to, she'd humiliated him, or so the newspapers had reported almost daily in his absence, alleging, in one form or another, that *she* was now the Emperor of Mexico, that it was she who wore the trousers, not he.

"Certainly, the blow to her pride was significant. But for granting the occasional public audience or agreeing to tour some new orphanage or school, she kept mostly to herself here. She smiled, she entertained modestly, she did all she could to appear content with her life, though she'd been greatly wounded by her husband's rebuke. Yet it was the loneliness that hurt her most, for you see by then the two of them were leading all but separate lives. He'd given up horseback riding and no longer went swimming with her in the secret pond they'd discovered in the woods here, where, according to legend, Malinche, the famous mistress of Cortés, used to bathe. He seemed to have lost his affection for Chapultepec altogether, often spending the nights in his rooms in the city, where he liked to eat and drink with his friends. When he wasn't working, he was touring the provinces or cultivating his private interests (the nature of which she was loath to imagine) in his lavish retreat in Cuernavaca, colloquially known as La Casa de Olvido or The House of Forgetting, for, though he'd built a special cottage on the grounds for his young Indian lover, he'd forgotten to build one for his wife! Do you remember the Borda Gardens?"

"Yes, they were lovely," I replied. "I remember them well, the terraces and fountains. I remember talking about Lowry."

"Yes, poor man! I remember that, too. In any case, Maximilian spent more and more time there in Cuernavaca on his own, sometimes remaining there for weeks at a time, where (so we now know) he tended his peacocks, drank tequila, and enjoyed the nightly favors of the seventeen-year-old Indian girl with whom he'd fallen in love. Of course, Carlota was wretched without him, retreating further and further into herself. She read less, wrote fewer letters, and finally gave up horseback riding altogether, a past-time that had always been dear to her. She became haughty, impatient, and cold. Her beautiful smile vanished.

"Then things got worse. One day, as the pressure mounted for her to produce an heir to the throne, Maximilian announced his decision to adopt one instead. It was then that the gossips really set to work on her, both here and abroad, accusing her of being frigid, of being sterile, of denying the Emperor his conjugal dues. One writer, in a popular Italian newspaper, surmised that her problem was anatomical: her vagina was too small. That and more she endured in silence in the hope that her beloved Maximilian would return to her one day, that once again he would seek out her love.

"Finally, just when she thought all was lost, Maximilian offered her the chance to redeem herself." We had entered the main gallery of the museum and for a few moments stood speechless before the great Sun Stone, a relic we'd seen together before, and had talked about at length (the sun god Tonatiuh, the human hearts in his sharply clawed hands), when softly, leading me away from the crowd that had gathered there, a Chinese couple, a large Mexican family, a few backpackers, and what appeared to be a tour of elderly Israelis, Arsène continued, "Her charge, her mission, was simple: she was to travel to France, to Paris, to persuade Napoleon III not to withdraw his troops from Mexico, on which troops the monarchy depended in its struggles against Juárez.

"Yet it was hardly a simple charge. Some believe that Maximilian set her up to fail, that he knew she would never succeed. Still, the young empress was not to be deterred; fired by hope, by a determination to prove herself true to him, and to Mexico itself, she began her preparations at once.

"As you can imagine, the journey from Veracruz to Saint-Nazaire was long and hard," he explained. "Crossing the Atlantic back then took nearly a month, during which time the empress read widely, kept a travel log, and studied the captain's maps. What's more, she dedicated long hours to their plans for the mission before her, carefully reviewing the instructions her husband had rehearsed with her—the feints, the arguments, the very tones of voice she should use. For nothing could be left to chance. For the stakes had never been higher: she knew that her interview with Napoleon III would determine not only the fate of their empire, but the fate of their marriage as well."

At that point he smiled, then sighed, and for an instant I glimpsed the man I'd known. How I'd loved him! Shaking his head, he said, "The interview did not go well. She found Napoleon an ugly, broken old man. While gallant as ever (for Charlotte was still a beautiful young woman), his kidney stones had taken their toll on him. His hands trembled; he grimaced; he sat hunched like a cripple at his desk. To make matters worse, he seemed unable to focus on her, preoccupied as he was with the rise of Bismarck and Prussia, a development, a resurgence, which he himself had endorsed. Mexico—which he'd already abandoned under pressure from the United States—was the last thing on his mind.

"Still Charlotte made her plea; she'd worked too hard and traveled too far to quit on the country now. Adhering strictly to her husband's plan, she insisted to the emperor that she and Maximilian had not failed in Mexico, not at all, that their continued struggles with Juárez had more to do with insufficient funding, and with the rank incompetence of the French commander, Bazaine, than with their vision and rule. This she argued with vigor, and at length, as she'd been coached to do, presenting the weary sovereign with document after document in substantiation of their cause, each of which she knew by heart, yet which he only waved away, as if swatting at flies, finally dismissing her with the promise that he would discuss the matter with his ministers as soon as he felt better.

"She knew what that meant. In a letter to Maximilian, written shortly thereafter, she cursed the wretched old man, describing in fine detail the way she'd demolished his arguments, one by one, to expose him for the fraud and coward he was, a letter she concluded by declaring him the very Devil himself.

"Deeply discouraged, she retreated to Miramare, in Trieste, where, in a fit of pique, she decided to celebrate the Mexican national holiday there in all its pomp and glory! On the morning of September 16th, the people of the city were awakened at dawn by a volley of gun salutes fired from the Austrian fleet, then anchored offshore. Puzzled, excited, they hurried to the park at Miramare, the beautifully maintained gardens of which had been decked out in Mexican colors, to glimpse the empress herself and to hear the Austrian orchestra playing Mexican songs!"

Upon his lead, I followed him into another one of the galleries, the museum's extensive exhibit on the

Maya, where we stood for time before a ceremonial bowl in the shape of a conch shell out which a grinning old man had just popped his head—or such was its effect on us, its appeal. "See the earrings there; he must be a priest!" he exclaimed, when once again he was familiar to me, Arsène, if but briefly, for when he spoke again he seemed changed.

"Angry, flustered, as she was after her meeting with Napoleon, the empress was not to be deterred. For she had a plan, a plan she'd devised on her own. Not long after the celebration at Miramare, she set out for Rome in the hope of currying favor with the pope, Pope Pius IX, who'd agreed to meet with her to talk about the future of Mexico, a matter of considerable interest to him. Passing by coach and train through Mantua and Bologna, she arrived in Rome in late September of 1866. There, at the train station, she was met by a delegation of cardinals, members of the Roman aristocracy, and a unit of Papal Swiss Guards in sparkling breastplates, before being led through the streets of the city with great pomp and ceremony to the Albergo di Roma, where an entire floor had been reserved for her. This more gracious welcome seemed to bode well for her plans.

"Her first interview was with the formidable Cardinal Antonelli. Much to her surprise, he agreed at once to the idea of forming a pact with the Mexican empire. It seemed to him a matter of course, though he was concerned by Maximilian's proclamation of religious tolerance there, a leniency he felt opened the door to all sorts of heresy. Her interview with the pope himself followed shortly thereafter. Dressed in black, according to the custom, she, in the company of her Mexican entourage, climbed the steps to the second floor of the Vatican palace on the appointed day, preceding slowly past the grand master of the Holy Hospice, the grand squire, the assistants to the throne, and the marshal of the Holy Church, and finally entering the Throne Room itself where she found the pope seated placidly on a gold and red throne. He rose at once to greet her. When he held out his ring for her to kiss it, all of her fears and frustrations coalesced at once: 'Holy Father, save me!' she cried. 'I have been poisoned!'

"You can imagine his surprise," said Arsène, before I had a chance to respond, to express my amazement. "Oh, to have seen his face!"

"So, what happened?" I asked. "What did he say?"

"He didn't say anything. At least not directly. He simply pretended he hadn't heard her. Instead, he himself raised the matter of Mexico and her mission there to see him, of which he'd been duly informed, insisting straightaway, before she could even begin to make her case to him, that he needed to consult the Mexican bishops before considering an accord of any kind. And like that," he said, snapping his fingers, "her audience was over."

"God, she must have been devastated."

"Yes, surely—the beginning of the end. At least that's what my late friend, the writer Fernando del Paso believed, that that was the turning point for her, the point at which her madness set in: 'I, insane? The Baroness of Nothing, the Princess of Foam, the Queen of Oblivion?' Brilliant, isn't it? It's from his novel, *Noticias del Imperio.*"

"You knew Del Paso?" Some time ago I'd read his novel *Palinuro de México* and had liked it very much.

"Yes, it's funny, I was in Librería Regia one day, browsing the collection there, when, strange thing, we reached for the same book, the Bibliothèque de l'Image edition of the still life paintings of the 17th century Italian painter, Giovanna Garzoni. Have you heard of her? Of course, I recognized him at once, Del Paso—his white hair, his large glasses, his brightly colored suit. I told him I was a psychiatrist from New York and that I was writing a psycho-historical diagnosis of the Empress Carlota. He thought the idea ridiculous. 'To what end?'

he cried, there in the crowded bookstore, a question to which I responded at length, when later we sat drinking brandy in a rooftop restaurant nearby. While he ate, I talked and drank, though I've never liked brandy. When I finished telling him about my book he burped at me, then shook his head. 'You're either an idiot or some very rare strain of genius,' he told me. After that, we sometimes met there for lunch, with its splendid view of the cathedral and of the ruins of Templo Mayor, to talk about history and books, which wasn't very often, truth be told, for by then he was living in Guadalajara.

"In any case, the empress was staggered by this blow to her mission. For days she didn't set foot outside her suite at the Albergo di Roma, eating nothing but nuts and oranges, the peels of which she littered the floors. Then one morning she burst from her rooms and ordered a coach to take her at once to the Trevi Fountain where she scooped up the water in her hands and drank greedily, for by then she was severely dehydrated, only to climb back into the coach crying, 'To the Vatican! To the Vatican!'

"At first the pope refused to speak with her, but finally relented. Upon seeing him at his breakfast, the desperate woman snatched the steaming cup of chocolate from his hands and drank it down. 'I am so hungry!'

she despaired, 'But I don't dare eat—they are all trying to poison me!'

"When the pope offered her her own cup of chocolate she replied, 'No, I only want to drink out of Your Holiness's cup; if they know it is for me, they will put poison in it, I am sure.'

"Naturally, the pontiff was flabbergasted; he knew that she could not be treated like any ordinary lunatic, but had to be soothed and pampered until proper arrangements could be made. It was his idea to distract her with some old manuscripts from his library, which proved successful, allowing him to slip away unnoticed. At length, upon a proposal that she visit the Vatican gardens, something she'd always wanted to do, the empress allowed herself to be led away, then was driven back to her suite at the Albergo di Roma, where for a time she slept peacefully, only to wake in hysterics that afternoon, demanding to be driven back to the Vatican, the only place in the world she felt safe. Once readmitted, she refused to leave, demanding that she be allowed to spend the night there, something no woman had ever done in the history of the Church!"

"What a story. So, what did the pope do?" I asked, following Arsène out into the sunlight again.

"Remarkably, he agreed to allow her to stay for one

night there, as long as she was out by the morning. By that time, he hoped to have made other, more suitable arrangements for her care, as she was clearly deranged. In the meantime, he saw to it that two copper beds were brought up to the library for her and her lady-in-waiting, a kind and dutiful woman named Madam del Barrio."

"Incredible!"

"Yes, truly," he agreed. "Yet the story gets stranger still. Once settled in the Vatican, in her makeshift suite there, the empress demanded that she be served her dinner at once, for she was ravenous, nearly wild-eyed with hunger, though even there, in the safety of the pope's own library, she refused to touch the food, once it arrived, that is, unless the pope himself was willing to feed it to her!"

"And did he?"

"He did. There, surrounded by bishops and other dignitaries, he spoon-fed the empress of Mexico as though she were a child!"

At that point he broke off his story, suggesting we get a cup of coffee and sit for a while in the museum cafe. Unfortunately, all of the tables were occupied, so we had to wait for a while to be seated. When finally we ordered and were served (he a roll of some sort and coffee and me a ham sandwich with a glass of iced tea), he asked, "Do you remember that little restaurant called Chumley's? You know, over in the West Village there on Bedford? I think you were the one who first took me there. Yes, I'm sure of it."

I didn't remember that, though I remembered the place itself, a refurbished old speakeasy that had been popular with students. "Of course," I replied. "We went there a lot. Usually drank too much!" He chuckled at the remark, though without smiling, for he was clearly preoccupied. "What made you think of it?"

He shrugged his shoulders. "I really don't know. The other night I suddenly remembered the time, many years later, when I took Simin there." He sipped his coffee and frowned. "We were sitting at a little table like this one, it was snowing outside, there was a fire in the fireplace, and I remember she was angry, angry at me, she hated the food there, the noise, when apropos of something, she turned to me and said: 'You get what you deserve, you know. Everyone does.'"

It was then that he looked at me, a long, probing look. I felt the blood rush to my face, and was about to stammer something, anything to divert him, when he said, "Do you believe it's true?"

"That what's true?"

"That we get what we deserve."

There it was at last, the challenge I'd be waiting for—and I hated him for it. I wanted to take his head in my hands and bash it against the table. I wanted to cover the floor with his brains and blood. For suddenly it was clear to me that, ever since we met that morning, he'd been planning the moment when he'd confront me at last, carefully gauging his timing, his words. All that talk about the empress and Candela! I felt sick with loathing for him, for the way he'd set me up, for the way he'd led me straight into his trap. I thought of the times I'd defended him to Simin, of the occasions I'd praised him to her, making excuses for his habits, his ways. What's more, I'd urged Simin to speak to him. Many times. I'd begged her to be frank with him, to tell him the truth. It was the least she could do.

And of course I'd warned her about David. Again and again I'd warned her about him, I'd told her to beware.

Sitting there with Arsène, I trembled with rage. I wanted to shake him by the collar, to cry, "And what about *me*? The guilt, the anguish! And for what? Simin and David used me, trapped me. How am I of all people to blame?" I wanted to spit in his face.

"I haven't the faintest idea," I said at length—apparently so tersely, so dismissively, that he cocked his head at me. Then a strange mood passed over his face. He lifted his cup then set it down again. "Shall we go?"

OUTSIDE, HE LOOKED ABOUT HIM, as if trying to orient himself in the bright spring light. He appeared genuinely confused. It seemed I'd misread him, his intentions, misjudged what he'd said, for he didn't even look at me, but staggered off toward Paseo de la Reforma and Chapultepec Lake.

Abashed, I followed him at a distance, struggling to fathom what had just happened, what it was he'd expected me to say.

From behind, he looked smaller, older to me, his shoulders slumped, his bearing disjointed, his manner oddly, strangely discomposed. He stopped to pet a dog and nearly collided with a man on a bicycle who cursed him roundly before pedaling off through the crowd. When I caught up with him I was surprised to find him weeping.

"What is it?" I said, taking him by the arm and leading him across the busy avenue, for he refused to stop walking. "Was it something I said?"

"You never said anything," he replied, ambiguously, only to snort impatiently, "Don't you see?"

I braced myself, felt my mouth go dry. "See *what*?" I exclaimed, for my wits were at an end.

He looked at me; he was trembling. "That I trusted her. I trusted her to *know!*"

"To know what? I don't understand!"

"To warn me, of course! She knew I was trying. We'd talked about it! She knew I had trouble with the signs."

"What signs?" I demanded. I was thoroughly confused.

"The signs, the signs! They're everywhere!" he despaired, waving his arms about him where we'd stopped on the crowded path. "If only I'd seen them... If only I'd known..."

When I touched him on the arm he started, as if shaken from a dream, then hurried off down the path again, walking swiftly this time, so that I followed him until he stopped at the tip of the lake again in order to get his bearings. He looked at the paddle boats, he nodded at two boys chasing a pigeon, only to be distracted by the packages of garishly colored cotton candy for sale at one of the food carts beside him. I saw him check his watch, when, as if suddenly taken with an idea, he continued on along the path by Lago menor, walking quickly enough that I had to jog to keep pace with him.

He'd walked perhaps a hundred yards along the lake when he stopped again, turned back to me, and cried, "Look! You can see the castle from here!"

The change in him was as sudden as it had been just minutes before. Talking, smiling, he seemed himself again and laughed.

FROM THERE TO THE BASE OF THE CASTLE was but a short stretch, and soon we found ourselves crowding our way into the grounds through the fine, wrought-iron gates. It had been years since I'd visited the castle, and suddenly I yearned to see the city from there, from high above the trees.

The climb up the wide, winding ramp was longer and steeper than I remembered it, so that frequently we were forced to pause along the balustrade to catch our breath. Once at the top, we didn't bother to go inside the palace, we had toured the rooms and museum before, but made our way through the crowds of tourists at the entrance, to Arsène's favorite place on the wide, open terrace, with its pergolas and statues and lushly potted flowers, where we stood at the parapet, looking out over the old gatehouse, in the direction of Condesa.

"The empress never saw this view again," he remarked, once he'd collected himself, wiping his brow and lips with his handkerchief. His normally wan cheeks were flushed from the exertion. "At least the view as it was then."

"So, she never returned from her trip?"

"No, she never saw her husband again, but died alone at Bouchout Castle in Belgium. By then she was stark raving mad."

"What happened after her night at the Vatican? Where did she go from there?" I asked him, directing him to an empty bench where we could sit, for it was far too warm to stand in the sun.

"From there?" he mused. "Why, she had nowhere to go but back to Miramare, in Trieste." At that point, he opened his pack, rummaged around inside it, then closed it again with a frown, finally setting it on the ground beside him, so that I couldn't help wondering what it was he'd been looking for, what trinket, what book, when, as if having reconciled himself to the fact of its absence, he remarked, "Foucault says that language is the first and last structure of madness. I'd hoped to show you the passage from his book, to read it aloud to you, but in my haste to meet you this morning I seem to have left it behind. No matter. Still it would have been nice to have shared it with you. I was looking forward to your reaction."

"Well, what was the gist if it?" I pressed him. "Perhaps you can describe it to me." I liked it better when he was talking.

"That's the thing: it's hard to piece together. I can't claim to understand it at all, except to say that it somehow rings true to me. Do you know what I mean?"

"Yes, I've read many things like that, things that, though I feel I've grasped them in some way, at some level, I could never explain. Not even to myself."

"Exactly!" he cried, squeezing my arm. "More and more that seems the case with me, that I understand things in a way I could never explain."

He smiled, a crooked weary smile, then gave my arm another squeeze. "Forgive me, you asked me about the empress, about what she did after her night at the Vatican."

"You said she returned to Miramare."

"Yes, but not at once. When she awoke the next day in her makeshift quarters, there in the Vatican, her lady-in-waiting, Madam del Barrio, noticed that she was much calmer, as if the night had resolved some of the puzzles in her brain. Once dressed, she asked for paper and a writing set. To Madam del Barrio she said: 'I have been poisoned and am going to die.' Without another word, she wrote four short letters, each dated October 1, 1866: the first to her husband, 'her beloved treasure'; two to the pope; and one, the shortest of all, a sort of preface to her will, addressed to no one in particular, in which she declared that she did not want her body to be laid out after her death. Rather, she wanted to be buried simply in the church of Saint Peter, in the habit of the Clarissian nuns, and as close as possible to the Holy Apostle's tomb."

"Buried simply!"

"That's what she wrote." He shrugged his shoulders, shook his head—whether in amazement or pity I couldn't tell. "And that was that. She rose from the desk, commanded Madam del Barrio to have her coach brought round, then gathered her things, eager to get back to her hotel."

"Was it then that she returned to Miramare?"

"Sadly no, for once again her condition worsened, so that she spent the next five days locked in her room, ranting and raving and accusing everyone in her delegation of trying to kill her, of being agents of Napoleon III. If anything, her paranoia worsened. Day after day, night after night, she paced the rooms, unwilling or unable to sleep, certain that any moment she would die. Yet she didn't die. Not then, not there. She grew hungry and thirsty, terribly thirsty, all the while refusing to eat or drink.

"It was a woman named Mathilde Doblinger, who also had traveled with her from Mexico City, who devised the plan of buying a few live chickens, a small coal oven, and a basket of eggs, so that the empress could oversee the preparation of her meals each day, and thus be reassured they were safe." At that point he grinned, his face awash with amazement.

"What?" I asked. "What?"

"Why, the description of her room there! I wish I had the passage with me to read to you."

"Well, what was it like, her room? Was there something strange about it?"

"No, the room itself was ordinary enough, if larger than most, with tall, curtained windows opening out onto the Corso. What distinguished it, that is, after a few days, was that the carpet was covered with feathers and blood!"

"Of course! They must have slaughtered the chickens right there."

"Yes, you can imagine the smell, for by then the heat of the city was stifling."

"How long did that continue? Surely not for long."

"No, not for much longer," replied Arsène. "One day, no doubt oppressed by her confinement there, if not by the stench alone, the empress sent a telegram to her favorite brother, Philippe, demanding that he come to her rescue in Rome. That done, she demanded to speak with Maximilian's Mexican butler, a man named Blasio, who had traveled with her to Europe, as per her husband's secret order. She wished to dictate to him a number of important decrees, as she knew that his penmanship and spelling were good. When he entered her room, having expected to find a lunatic still tearing at her hair and clothes, he found her beautifully dressed and groomed, the very picture of courtly restraint.

"Still, by then the change in her was plain. As he scratched away at the paper, he studied her thin, drawn face, inwardly appalled by her protruding cheekbones and by her eyes, which gleamed with a bizarre and feverish light. The bed, he noticed, with its silken canopy, had not been slept in. He saw the blood, the feathers. He saw the small oven in which her meals were cooked, her nightstand with its gold watch and half-burned candle, and the small table at which she sat to eat her meals, to one leg of which a pair of softly clucking chickens were tethered with twine."

"So, what was the nature of the decrees? Did she have any real power at all?"

"No, not as such. As best I understand it, they were decrees of destitution for various members of her entourage and staff, relieving them of all titles and duties forthwith. For that she still had the authority. She simply didn't trust them anymore. By then, she'd placed all of her hope in her brother."

"Did he ever reply to her telegram?"

"He did more than that; though filled with appre-
hension, and timorous by nature, he arrived in Rome
the very next day. Much to his relief there was not a
hint of madness about her. You must understand that
by then there was hardly anyone in Europe who wasn't
talking about her."

"And did he take her away?"

"No, for again her plans had changed. After
meeting him at the train station, there by the old
Baths of Diocletian, she took him for a ride through
the city instead, for a tour of the sites, as he'd never
seen Rome before."

"He must have been baffled, poor man."

"No doubt he was. After all, how could all of the
newspapers be wrong? Certainly, he was scratching his
head, for he found his sister lovelier, livelier than ever,
pointing this way and that, and generally impressing
him with her knowledge of architecture, art, and history.
Together, and in the days that followed, they saw the
Pantheon, the Forum, the Trevi Fountain, and the Sistine
Chapel. They visited the Borghese Gardens and those of
the Pincio (or collis hortorum), once the famous gardens
of Lucullus. They even climbed the 137 steps of the Scala
di Spagna to see the church of the Santissima Trinità dei
Monti, poised there like a crown at the top. It seemed she

was particularly fond of the Colosseum, which she'd seen one night by the light of the moon. Did you know that in 1855 there were 420 varieties of plants growing there?"

"In the Colosseum?"

"Yes, though there are probably no more than 20 or 30 now." He nodded thoughtfully to himself, scratched his chin, then removed his glasses to polish them. "Sometimes I miss it, Rome—the noise, the traffic, that 'compost of civilized time'. Of course, there is plenty of that here, isn't there? Perhaps that's why I like it so much. I've always felt the Mexicans and Romans were kin."

Rising to his feet, he chuckled, as if struck by some intrigue. "Did you ever see the portraits of Benito Juarez and his wife, Margarita Maza, the ones inside here?" he asked me, indicating the museum behind us.

"I don't remember. Why?" All I remembered were the carriages.

"The last time I was here I was taken by the fact that they have the same expression on their faces, the very same look in their eyes. Even their lips are the same."

"Were they painted by the same artist? That might explain it."

"Perhaps," he replied, "though it might be something else."

"Like what?"

"Like…" he began, when he stopped himself. "No, better yet, let's have a look at them together and you yourself can decide!"

The portraits, hung side by side, just inside the museum entrance, were difficult to make out for all of the people clustered there. In time, however, we were able to assume a position directly before them.

Sure enough, Arsène was right: their expressions were remarkably similar, so much so that I had to get very close to them to notice the differences, albeit fairly subtle ones. They had the same thin, determined lips, the same dark, unwavering eyes.

I felt him hesitate beside me when at last, having restrained himself for some minutes, he said, "From what I've read they were very much in love."

"That's funny, they don't look like they're in love." I couldn't resist it. "They look like they've been fighting."

"And so they do! I see that now. She was probably sick of him running all around the country, killing French soldiers. Do you know that she and her children spent the duration of the Second Mexican Empire living in exile in Washington, D.C.? As the First Lady of Mexico, she met frequently with Abraham Lincoln and the gracious, if long-suffering Mary Todd. For she too suffered terribly from depression."

"Why *too*?" I asked.

"Too?" he murmured. "I meant in addition to the empress herself, as it is clear to me that she also suffered from the disease, the particulars of which I explore at some length in my book."

"So, what is it that puzzles you about the portraits?" Apart from their likeness, I still didn't understand. "What is it you'd started to tell me?"

Briefly he thought about it, then waved it away. "Nothing, really. Never mind. What do you say we get a drink somewhere, as it's getting late? Find something a bit more substantial to eat."

The suggestion was welcome, as my feet ached and I was feeling generally weary. It had been a while since I'd walked for so long.

ONCE OUT OF THE park, we took a taxi to a restaurant in Condesa he liked. It was a handsome, airy place with wooden tables and chairs, rustic wood flooring, and a fine wooden bar with a copper railing where we seated ourselves on the short-backed stools at one end. He ordered a bottle white burgundy and a dish of roasted eggplant, tomatoes, and anchovies for us to share. "You'll love it," he assured me, sipping his wine and sighing. "The place is at its best right now, when they open up all of the windows and doors. Some nights I sit here for hours."

It pleased me to see that he was back to his garrulous old self, chatting easily with the bartenders and waiters, who clearly knew him and were accustomed to his ways. He seemed at home there in the restaurant, and in the city itself—at least more so than he'd ever seemed in Manhattan. It was something I envied in him.

By that time, I was far more tired than I thought, a fact soon brought home to me by the wine and the food, which made me drowsy, so drowsy in fact that I thought of excusing myself and returning to my apartment to sleep. I had a lot of work to do before flying back to New York on Thursday, so that it was important I feel rested in the morning.

Sipping his wine, Arsène was telling me, and anyone else who would listen, the story of a long and wretched week he'd spent with Simin in a cabin they'd rented on Yunuén Island in the middle of Lake Pátzcuaro one fall. He was so happy in the telling of it that I was loath to interrupt him.

That he still loved her was plain, so plain, so piteous, that at points I actually winced at his description of their week there together. For all I knew, she'd never really loved him at all.

At length, he ordered another bottle of wine, our third, as well as a small roasted chicken and an octopus curry, when I took the opportunity to distract him by asking him to tell me more about the empress, whose tale he hadn't finished telling.

"The empress, eh?" he said, tearing off one of the chicken's tiny drumsticks. "I should have you run your eyeballs over the first few chapters again and tell me what you think."

"Yes, I'll be happy to. You can send them to me tomorrow." He made me help myself to some of the chicken before remarking, "Poor, poor woman. So much smarter than that husband of hers. Just look at any photo of him—so ugly, so clearly inbred!"

"How long did she and her brother remain in Rome?"

He paused for a moment, sipped his wine, when in a rush it all came back to him. "For a week or so, I believe. They had a splendid time together. At least at the start. They visited the museums and galleries, they listened to music, they even hired horses and rode out across the flats and dells of the Campagna together, stopping to eat a picnic lunch in the open arch of one of the crumbling aqueducts there, as in a scene from *The Marble Faun.*" He looked positively wistful.

"Then one day…." he began, briefly raising a finger, so that he could have another sip of wine, "one day when they were having lunch together in her room, after a morning spent walking and talking, the empress, suddenly glaring at the dishes arrayed between them on the table, said, 'I'll tell you everything, my chubby boy!' For that is what she called her brother. And that was when things changed for the worse.

"From the table she picked up a little knife covered with dried ink." Instinctively Arsène did the same, taking up a butter knife and pointing at its blade. "'You see, that is strychnine,' she said. 'And it's not just me, they're after, my chubby boy, but you, too. Think of mother and father, Lord Palmerston, and Prince Albert—all of them poisoned, murdered by that Antichrist, Napoleon III!"

I hadn't expected such a reversal and now was fully awake.

"That night Philippe stayed with her in her room at the Albergo di Roma. He was gravely concerned for her, if not a little anxious about the things she'd said. Could any of it be true? he wondered. He doubted it, and still he fretted, as she paced the room before him, speaking restlessly, feverishly of Mexico, that magical word 'Mexico', of the scenery and people, and of the palaces she would build there, when again the litany of poisonings would begin."

All the while I studied Arsène. His own eyes seemed feverish now, his hair was tousled, his mouth had gone slack. He grinned, he nodded, occasionally he squeezed my arm. "I'm glad we're together again," he told me, at one point. "It's been years, you know. Of course, things can never be the same."

"It's good to see you, too, Arsène. Really good. To think, I might have missed you altogether on this trip."

"That's true!" he exclaimed, only to cock his head at me. I noticed that he couldn't hold it still. "I was wondering about that. Why *did* you call me anyway? How did you know I was here?"

"I didn't. I had no idea. I guess I just felt like talking."

"Well, we've talked now, haven't we? And what a talk it's been! Why, I can't remember having talked with anyone this way in years. I must admit I've been feeling quite lonely." Briefly, he tried to get the bartender's attention, when he said, "Do you remember back in college when we used to sit there in Tompkins Square Park with our cigarettes and beer and just chat the night away? It didn't matter what we said, only that we were sitting there and talking like there was no one else in the world."

"Yes, I remember it. I remember it well."

He shrugged his shoulders, sipped his wine. "Then of course we went our separate ways. It was bound to happen," he said with a frown, when he clapped me on the back. "Yet here we are again! Amazing. It's something to be grateful for."

I wanted to say more, to tell him everything—that I was sorry for having betrayed him, sorry for having remained silent all these years, but the words just wouldn't come. Yet did it really matter, the truth? I didn't think so. What good would it do him now? Unwilling to drink any more, I ordered coffee for us, along with a chocolate tart, so that it took only the slightest prompting to get him to finish his tale about the empress.

"Sad to say, things went from bad to worse. The empress refused to eat at all, even with her brother's assurances, shrieking and crying and throwing the dishes and silverware out the window, for she was certain they too had been tainted.

"Apparently one day, having woken from a brief nap and spotting a pot of stew on the stove, she plunged her hand into the boiling liquid and extracted a large hunk of meat, which she tried to devour on the spot before the pain overwhelmed her.

"It was only after days of pleading and cajoling, when

she had all but wasted away for lack of nourishment, that her brother was able to get her to board a train to Trieste, when soon thereafter he saw her safely settled at Miramare.

"Such a beautiful place it was—and is," he added, pensively, "though one senses there's something not quite right about it. Twice I've been there, to Miramare, and each time I've had the same strange feeling. In any case it was there, in the spacious ground-floor apartments that she was kept under lock and key."

"Was she still in touch with her husband?"

"No, not really. Not wanting to distress him any more than necessary, given all he was dealing with at the time, they withheld her letters to him, most of which were gibberish anyway, simply reassuring her that he loved her very much and would soon join her there, when, if all went well, he would take her back to Mexico."

"Which of course wasn't true," I said.

"No, it wasn't true, but it seemed to calm her some, for her prognosis was not good. At least according to her doctors there. Maximilian's physician Dr. Jilek and the respected alienist Professor Riedel agreed about that, convinced she was suffering from insanity with a persecution complex, to paraphrase their diagnosis. In truth, they were fumbling in the dark for an explanation of her condition, which seemed to change from day to day, at one point blaming her illness on the climate and conditions of Mexico (the air, the water, the spicy food), then on her failed negotiations with Napoleon III, then on her husband's notorious impotence, on the fact that in all their years together they'd never once had sex. Some say he'd never even touched her, but formally."

"So, he actually was impotent?"

"Who knows? What's clear is that he was unfaithful to her—in what form I cannot say. Surely that was painful enough." He hung his head for a moment, when soberly he looked about him. He was surprised to find that the restaurant was nearly empty, though it was only half past eight.

"Naturally, the empress didn't take things lying down, but fought their restrictions, tooth and nail, punching and kicking them, when they came to examine her, even escaping her apartments once or twice, until they were forced to move her to the nearby Castelleto, where they had the doors replaced and the windows nailed shut.

"Their subsequent routine for her was as simple as it was strict: she was awakened between seven and eight each morning, served a breakfast of coffee and rolls, given a bath in warm water, then encouraged to listen to music and draw, which familiar pastimes they believed would soothe her heart and mind. Weather permitting, she was allowed to take a walk under escort in the gardens. Lunch was served punctually at one-thirty, after which she was permitted another stroll. During the evenings she was encouraged to read or play cards before her bedtime at nine o'clock sharp. From the reports I've read, she rarely ventured out of her rooms in the Castelleto, but spent her days sitting at her window, gazing blankly at the sea."

"And what about Maximilian? How much did he know about her and her condition?"

"Surely by that point he knew that she was gravely ill. It seemed he'd loved her after all, as he'd attested in numerous letters to her, most of which had been withheld from her for fear they would agitate her blood. Unbeknownst to her, he'd recently made plans to set sail for Europe to see her, a prospect she'd dreamt of nearly every day since her return to Miramare."

"So, what prevented it?" I asked.

"The war. In particular, the sudden withdrawal of French troops. That was early February, 1867. You see, without the aid of French troops Maximilian didn't stand a chance against Juárez."

"Then why did he stay?"

"Pride, vanity, I suppose. Or maybe just madness.

Who can say? Even after Mexico City had fallen to the republican forces, when he'd retreated with a coterie of his generals to the city of Querétaro, which city was also soon surrounded, he refused to give up, to lay down his arms, let alone to accept Juárez's offer to grant him safe passage out of Mexico. He was stubborn that way. Even after he'd been forced to surrender, when imprisoned and laid low by dysentery, he'd remained defiant. Nothing could break his spirit, nothing, that is, except the news, whispered to him by one of his cellmates one day, that his beloved wife Charlotte was dead."

"But she wasn't dead, was she?"

"No, she died much later, in Belgium, having outlived him by nearly sixty years!"

"Well, did she ever learn about his death? At some point she must have assumed it."

"Yes, she did, while living there at Bouchout Castle. It was a priest she knew who finally broke the news to her, who told her that her husband had lost the war against Juárez and been executed. That their reign in Mexico was over."

"And how did she respond?"

"At first with great restraint. She dressed herself in mourning, the black she was to wear for the rest of her life, took her usual walks, and made her usual visits into town. To all who condoled her she responded with dignity and sorrow."

"But then?"

Then she had a dream one night in which her husband Maximilian appeared to tell her he was not in fact dead, that it was not his corpse that had been sent to Europe but only a wooden likeness of him. What followed was an altogether different phase of her madness. More convinced than ever that people were trying to poison her, she suddenly isolated herself from everyone in order to devote herself to writing, which she did furiously, hour after hour, day after day."

"What was she writing?"

"Thoughts, mostly letters. She started writing and simply couldn't stop, covering thousands of sheets of paper with her script. While at first her handwriting was beautiful and clearly legible, for her penmanship was once elegant, it slowly became more and more cramped, more puzzling, finally deteriorating into a thicket of tiny, chicken-like scratches that were impossible to decipher, to read. Like a mystic, she wrote of invisible people in the room with her, of mysterious voices that whispered esoteric teachings to her. More than once she referred to her Maximilian as the Messiah. Then one day she suddenly declared that, from that moment on, she would no longer sign her name as Charlotte, but as Charles, for she claimed there were 'already three quarters of a man' in her. Her last note, signed Charles, read: 'I am the Pen of the world, for all I do is write.'

"In the years that followed, her life there at Bouchout Castle remained relatively uneventful. When it was raining, she could be seen pottering around in the hothouses or strolling alone through the park with its crisscrossing paths or sitting with a shawl around her shoulders in the fine English garden there, laid out decades before and faithfully maintained. She rarely wrote letters anymore, rarely interacted with anyone beside her doctors and the usual household staff. In the main she seemed placid, content.

"The gramophone was invented, then the vacuum cleaner, both of which delighted her. The Great War broke out, planes swept overhead and vanished. The great empires of Europe collapsed around her, the Bolsheviks seized control of the Kremlin, and more than a million soldiers lay dead or wounded on the banks of the Somme. Yet by then there was no room in her heart for any of it. There was not even room for God.

"Finally, on the morning of January 19th, 1927, after nearly sixty years of mourning, she took her last breath. At once Bouchout Castle, which had been closed to the world for decades, threw open its doors, so that people from near and far could file past her death-bed to pay their last respects."

IT WAS WELL AFTER NINE by the time we paid the bill and stepped outside. The air was warm and strangely fragrant as we wandered our way across the busy avenue and into the quiet backstreets of Condesa. He asked me what I had planned for the next day, when he told me he was thinking of taking a bus to have a look at Candela's Bacardí Rum Factory, now just a bottling plant, near the town of Izcalli.

I couldn't tell if he was asking me to join him or not, for he began at once to describe for me the innovative way in which Candela had used a different hypar form for the three original shells of the factory, that is, a different style of groined vault for each, for the cafeteria, the warehouse, and the parking canopy.

He was still talking about Candela when we reached the entrance to his building here.

Tired, we shook hands, when in the French fashion he kissed me on each cheek. Just as I turned to go he touched me on the arm. I'll never forget the look in his eyes. "So you knew all along," he said.

A couple passed us, laughing.

"Yes," I told him. "I knew it all along."

Acknowledgements

As ever I am grateful, deeply grateful, to the extraordinary Marc Estrin and Donna Bister for their work with me over the past four years. Their support and guidance have been invaluable to me.

I would like to thank Professor Rubén Gallo for his fascinating introduction to Gonzalo Celorio's novel, *And Let the earth Tremble at its Centers*. It was an inspiration to me. I am also indebted to the following books and their authors: *The Empress of Farewells: The Story of Charlotte, the Empress of Mexico* by Prince Michael of Greece; *The Crown of Mexico: Maximillian and His Empress Carlota* by Joan Haslip; *Maximilian and Carlota: Europe's Last Empire in Mexico* by M.M. McAllen; and the novel *News from the Empire* by Fernando Del Paso.

Finally, I would like to express my love and gratitude to the many friends and family members with whom I have wandered through the Chapultepec Parks of this world—George Ovitt, David Gutierrez, James Wolberg, Cynde Moore, Brendan Schallert, Ivan Hageman, Massimo Maglione, Tom Hurley, Steven Miglio, Hugh Himwich, Mickey Jones, Linda Forcey, Margaret Nash, Wes Rennie, Charles Forcey, Peter Forcey, my sons Ezra and Isaiah, and, of course, my wife and partner, Annie Nash, with whom I hope I never stop walking.

Peter Nash is the author of the novels, *Parsimony* and *The Perfection of Things*, and the biography, *The Life and Times of Moses Jacob Ezekiel: American Sculptor, Arcadian Knight.* He also co-authored a collection of essays called *Trotsky's Sink: Ninety-Eight Short Essays About Literature.* He lives in New Mexico with his wife and two sons.

Fomite
More novels and novellas from Fomite...

Fomite

Writing a review on social media sites for readers will help the progress of independent publishing. To submit a review, go to the book page on any of the sites and follow the links for reviews. Books from independent presses rely on reader-to-reader communications.

For more information or to order any of our books, visit:
http://www.fomitepress.com/our-books.html

CPSIA information can be obtained
at www.ICGtesting.com
Printed in the USA
FSHW020957070122
87483FS